Hollow Point

Eva Molenaar: Wartime Agent Book 4

by

Robert Craven

Cover Design by

Robert Craven 2017
using Canva app
www.canva.com

Table of Contents

Dedication

For Kim Much Emerson

Also by Robert Craven

Eva Molenaar: Wartime Agent Series

Get Lenin

Zinnman

A finger of Night

Eva Molenaar: Wartime Agent Book 4

1943

ONE

January 31st, Rastenburg, East Prussia

The onion soup had been carefully prepared from a recipe created by the Walterspiel brothers in Munich; a recipe created solely for him. The onions and ingredients came from the compound vegetable garden, grown and tended by the German horticultural firm, Zeidenspiner. Once the soup had been cooked by his personal chef, Otto Krümel, it was tasted by one of eleven women. The soup was served by his bodyguard, Rochus Misch, with a bottle of mineral water and a large warm slice of apple strudel.

The one thing Hitler hated above all else was weakness. He stared silently into his cooling winter onion soup. A throat was cleared and the message repeated.

"The German sixth army had offered terms to the Soviet forces at Stalingrad. Two hundred and seventy-five thousand men had been surrounded and crushed in less than six months by the Untermensch Asiatic hordes of the Red Army."

Unthinkable, as he had promoted and awarded General Friedrich Paulus, trapped in the city along with his troops, to the rank of Field Marshal.

Unbelievable, that instead of an honourable suicide befitting his new rank, the coward had surrendered and wanted to go to Moscow instead.

Hitler sent the soup back to the kitchens, untouched, but he devoured the strudel.

The nervous generals, Kurt Zeitzler, Alfred Jodl and Luftwaffe-General Hans Jeschonneck waited the following day for the daily midday conference; Hitler was an indolent man. Field Marshal Wilhem Keitel, Chief of operations at the OKW and Waffen SS Obersturmbannführer Viktor Bausch, Bormann's adjutant, stood silently with them.

"Strecker's XI corps are still fighting and holding the Northern pocket of Stalingrad, but his troops are running out of munitions and freezing to death," said Zeitzler, a bald, efficient man with a moustache similar to Hitler.

"He is to hold the Northern pocket, tie down as much of the enemy's resources as possible," said the Führer. His arm swept across the map of the city and surrounding country. He was now completely in charge of the war.

"With what, Führer?" said General Jodl.

Paulus and his staff had been sending desperate daily messages for months – "munitions coming to an end…munitions coming to an end." Luftwaffe-General Jeschonneck, groomed and polished, looked uncomfortable, the air support promised by Hermann Goering had never materialised. The medical evacuation flights out of the besieged city had been a blood-stained fiasco.

"Should we get a message to General Tojo?" he asked.

"Our forces will eradicate the Reds without their assistance!" said Obersturmbannführer Bausch. His eyes were a cold steel blue. His head was shaved to a pink razor burn. "This is an ideological conflict between races and we don't want our final victory with the Untermensch sullied with assistance from their kind!"

Jeschonneck sensed it was an inappropriate moment to mention that the Romanian divisions allied to the Germans had been smashed open by the Soviet forces.

Hitler felt life was the nation, and the nation had been betrayed by a weakling Field Marshal. Foreign journalists and film crews would soon be in Stalingrad to witness the first defeat of the invincible Wehrmacht. A substantial portion of the army and materiel was now gone, lost forever on the banks of the Volga, some two thousand miles away from Berlin.

"Strecker must hold out," said Hitler. "They are to fight to the last man."

"Führer, we must start considering options." Said Keitel.

"The German people mustn't know. That bastard Paulus!" The Führer was in an ecstasy of rage. As he phoned his personal adjutant, Julius Schaub, his left hand was shaking uncontrollably.

"Get me a line to Goebbels." He said.

"Von Ribbentrop should contact Stalin directly, through one of our embassies; Stockholm, maybe," suggested Jeschonneck.

"Offer terms? Capitulate! No not Goebbels, get me Speer now!"

With an effort, Hitler composed himself as the telephones began to ring in Berlin.

A fly started buzzing around the room, flitting about in the stale air.

"Do something about that bloody fly, Bausch," muttered Hitler.

"As it's flying shouldn't the Luftwaffe handle it, Führer?" smiled Bausch, nodding to Jeschonneck.

The Führer clenched his fists.

Bausch's demeanour slipped.

"Führer, I apologise.."

"Report to Himmler," said the Führer.

Bausch saluted straight armed.

"I have clowns for generals," said Hitler, "and I'm surrounded by clowns!"

The others followed Bausch outside. Jeschonneck muttered to Kietel and Jodl:

"The war is lost, Field Marshal. We should contact von Ribbentrop and start opening negotiations now," he looked back at the operations room door. "He said invading Russia would be like kicking down the door of a rotten structure, well he got that right, the whole blasted thing's come down on top of us. He's going to send us all to hell and he'll do it laughing his head off."

TWO

June, the Eastern Front, Russia

Commissar, 2nd rank of the Soviet Supreme General Staff, Valery Yvetchenko had been travelling for nearly thirty-six hours from Moscow. At Kursk's railway station, he watched the Soviet army's injured and dying waiting to be loaded onto evacuation trains. On the station wall someone had scrawled *'I am dying, but I am not surrendering'*. Blood seeped through the train's carriage doors onto the tracks. Yvetchenko's liaison, a young female pilot, made her way through the chaos, waving to him. Once he recognised her, she pointed toward the exit.

"Comrade Commissar, Yvetchenko, welcome, I am Troyanovskii, your pilot."

Outside the station, they stopped to watch an NKVD firing squad execute five bedraggled and injured soldiers. One nearly got out a plea for mercy before he was cut down.

"I see some won't be travelling home," said Yvetchenko.

"It's the punishment for dereliction of patriotic duty, Commissar."

It's a brave new world, he thought.

Troyanovskii flew the Yakovlev Yak-6 transport to what could be best described as a field. Then she escorted him to the waiting Stavka staff car. Her orders were to remain on standby.

Yvetchenko was a barrel-chested man. He had a pugilist's expression and flattened nose on which wire framed glasses perched uneasily. He was a precise man in every way.

The car, a battered lend-lease Studebaker bumped mercilessly along the rutted road.

"How much further, Comrade Zhuchkov?"

"Almost here, sir," replied the gaunt NKVD driver.

Yvetchenko spied the lines of Russian tanks and armoured cars up ahead. Loitering soldiers huddled in groups. At the sight of the Stavka staff car, they snapped to attention. A stern, ruddy-faced woman traffic controller waved it through. She saluted briskly as the car passed.

A haggard looking Commander opened Yvetchenko's door.

"Good morning, Commissar Yvetchenko, I am Commander Dimitry Plutenko, 28th Light Infantry," he was young, no more than twenty-five, with earnest blue eyes that already had seen too much war. A shock of blond hair crowned his high, unlined forehead. His uniform was tattered and stained and he looked as if he hadn't slept in days.

"What is it that you want Moscow to know about, Commander Plutenko?"

"Comrade Commissar, it has to be seen to be believed."

Past the lines of armour, they stood on a bluff.

"*This* was the 19th Infantry Regiment, Plutenko?"

As far as the eye could see, to the horizon, the earth was charred black to the gun metal grey of morning. Not a living thing was standing for miles around. The air gave off the miasma of a smelting works.

"We lost contact with them two days ago." Said Plutenko.

Men and horses had been stripped of their muscle and flesh; their blackened bones were had fused with the super-heated soil. Tanks, trucks, supply wagons and heavy weapons that had exploded, melted and cooled, now left jagged silhouettes.

"How many men?"

"Twelve thousand, nine hundred, Commissar. They were moving up to support the frontline, so there were probably additional auxiliary troops and vehicles."

"Survivors?"

"None, Commissar.'

Lighting a cigarette and inhaling the Oriental blend deeply, Yvetchenko scanned the horizon.

"Not even a bird in the sky" he said. The clouds seemed to inch their way around the sky; driven by different forces.

He spotted figures moving about in the distance,

"Who are they, Plutenko?"

"Penal unit. They were given a choice for their dereliction of patriotic duty: search for any survivors out there or firing squad. Personally, I'd have taken the bullet, Commissar."

An explosion boomed out across the wasteland, a plume of earth rose up, fanning outwards. It was followed by screams.

"One of the poor bastards must have stood on something," murmured Plutenko.

After a few moments, the wasteland was silent.

"Seems the Krauts have a new type of warhead, Commander Plutenko."

"They have nothing left after Stalingrad, Commissar."

"The German war machine is now a wounded beast, and wounded beasts are unpredictable and dangerous, Commander Plutenko."

Yvetchenko looked back at the lines of T-34 tanks.

"Who could let this slip?"

"Journalists from the Krasnaya Zvezda, our own troops, throw in local NKVD over there."

A veritable sieve, thought Yvetchenko.

"Take the journalists' cameras or notebooks. If they resist, shoot them on the spot."

"And..?" Plutenko nodded over to the cluster of NKVD; The People's Commissariat for Internal Affairs, Stalin's praetorian guard. They were taking photographs.

"Demand their cameras anyway; say it's on my orders. If they act up, threaten to have them shot too."

Yvetchenko finished his cigarette, stubbing the butt into the toxic soil. Where the butt had fallen a crystalline piece of soil caught his eye. He reached down and plucked it up. Holding it up towards the sun, light danced around it.

"Inform every soldier, signaller, commander and political officer, if they say anything about what's happened here, it's the gulag for the whole bloody lot of them. Understand?"

"I shall convey your orders, Commissar."

"Clearly, I hope."

Yvetchenko strode back to the car. The sun burst through the cloud cover and the summer heat began to rise.

"Get me to the airport, Zhuchkov."

Plutenko watched the battered car pitch and slide across the drying mud and spat onto the ground. He whistled over to the tank crews.

The engines started, belching black, acrid smoke across the land.

***

Yvetchenko's car, a lumbering black Zil, sped up the centre lane of the Leninsky prospekt; the lane reserved exclusively for the Politburo. It was the only vehicle on the road. The Kremlin's summer heat still lingered after midnight but was dissipated by the subterranean damp of the converted Kirovskaya metro station. In it, the Stavka's Great Patriotic War was being conducted from wooden desks partitioned off from each other by canvas sheets hanging from ropes and lines. The vast area smelled of cigarette smoke, sweat and old clothing. It boomed with shouted conversations.

Tugging aside the sheet that acted as a door, Yevtchenko shrugged off his greatcoat and threw it over his cot beside the desk. He debated whether or not to use the facilities here or at his private dacha in the nearby Dorogomilovo District. His body's most urgent needs won the day. In the toilet's cracked mirror, he didn't recognise the haggard reflection he was massaging water into. He needed a shave, a bath and a stiff drink; in reverse order.

Stretching out onto his cot fully clothed, he gingerly kicked off his sturdy Cossack boots; a perk of his party rank. Opening his tunic, he read the summons to the Kremlin for the dawn meeting about the annihilated 19th Infantry. Scanning down the page, he noted the threat issued by von Ribbentrop about the fate of Moscow. Then Yvetchenko fished out of the pile a directive from Molotov personally – it would seem that Commissar, 2nd rank of the Soviet Supreme General Staff, Yvetchenko would be travelling out of Mother Russia.

He re-read the directive; it was both a blessing and a death sentence at the same time; knowing Stalin's paranoia of external influence.

Reaching into this tunic, Yvetchenko pulled out the piece of toxic-looking, super-heated soil and looked at it one more time.

The threat from the Ribbentrop Bureau; the krauts had a new weapon.

He rose from the cot and pulled from the stack of coded correspondence an envelope. He placed the sample into it; he addressed it to The Academy of Sciences department to be delivered by special courier. On top of the pile, he spied a communique and brought it with him back to the cot.

The message he read before descending into fitful sleep was the real eye-opener; a man he thought long dead had appeared on the Russian/Romanian border. Rank, serial number and party card jumped out of the paper in his hand: Colonel Marko Kravchenko. The dead do rise, thought Yvetchenko, not once, not twice, but three times.

THREE
London

Peter de Witte's mews off Belgrave Road was usually darkened; the only illumination came from the windows once the black-out shades were drawn open. Today though, was different. He began his morning with a cigarette. His breathing was a little shorter after his bout of pneumonia; the chain smoking didn't help. He had positioned every piece of furniture precisely, allowing him to eschew his cane.

"Meeting's in an hour, Peter. I'll help you dress, if you want."

Martha de Witte helped him with his shirt. She had returned from neutral Ireland once notified by the service that he had been very seriously ill. They had been estranged since 1938. Martha was slim, tall and elegant and had never once stopped loving her husband. A man she had met while he was recuperating from being blinded by a grenade, introduced to her by section chief Henry Chainbridge nearly fifteen years ago.

"I'll get breakfast."

He held her face in his hands and tenderly ran his fingers along her features; she ran her fingers through his silver-flecked hair and kissed him gently.

"Coffee's just fine, thank you, darling." He said. He allowed his nose linger along her hair, bringing back distant sensory memories.

"Eat, you foolish man." She said.

Their moment was broken by the doorbell.

"Leave it." He whispered. He pulled her closer.

The doorbell jarred the silence.

"You're getting too old to be running around like this, Peter."

"Martha.."

She held a finger over his lips.

"Let's just see how things go for now, Peter; friends for now? Yes?"

He nodded ruefully.

"I have done some stupid things..."

"I know, Peter."

She kissed his forehead.

"Best not keep the powers that be waiting." She murmured.

His M.T.C. driver, Deborah Knox stood primly at the threshold. De Witte's friend and section chief, Henry Chainbridge, had insisted she be assigned to him, ensuring she had been issued and trained with a sidearm.

Martha de Witte watched her husband stumble a fraction before Knox steadied him.

No more adventures, she thought.

De Witte enjoyed the sun on his face as he found his pace and walked assuredly toward the staff car.

"The meeting's at Brompton Road this morning instead of Whitehall, because of a possible incoming air raid, sir."

Driver Knox's voice had a musical quality; she couldn't have been more than twenty. A little older than Eva Molenaaar when he had first met her, thought de Witte. Even after nearly a year since they had last spoken, his heart lurched and a dull ache spread slowly across his chest. He stopped and released a wracking cough.

"Is everything alright, sir?"

"Yes, Miss Knox, just a little wheezy, thank you," he dabbed his mouth delicately with a handkerchief, ensuring only a small corner of clean cloth appeared.

His senses told him that London was smashed in places, the acrid egg-smell of rubble, soiled water pipes, leaking gas mains and the faint undertow of death. Every vibration along the vehicle's chassis told him the roads were mashed up, in places pitted and pot-holed. Air raid sirens wailed in the far distance. Driver Knox dealt with the police and military roadblocks in a humorous, lively manner that always raised a laugh outside the cars window.

"I'll wait here for you, good luck, sir."

An armed Royal Navy sentry met him at the station door and nodded curtly at her.

The elevator plummeted down the four stories of Brompton Road to the Royal Navy Unit. Another armed sentry guided de Witte to the spacious office. From the surrounding offices typewriters and telemachines clattered and radio communications spat and hissed.

The meeting was with Minister of Information, Minister without portfolio and Special advisor to the PM, Brendan Bracken, and Special Operations Executive Director, Douglas Gageby.

"A 'uranium machine', fissile materials, Hydrogen, copper head," said Gageby as he flicked his eyes through the reports.

"Our dear friend, von Ribbentrop has recently issued an ultimatum to Stalin – Start peace negotiations now, on our terms, or the Reich will wipe Moscow from the face of the earth," said Bracken.

Gageby was uncertain as to why B.B., sworn 'privy council' to the PM, would be here sub-rosa; Bracken was a man steeped in subterfuge.

Gageby scanned the various memos, decrypted messages and reports, his eyes honed in on a strip of paper with the handwritten decryption – ++ **U-235 en-route from SouthAm ++ date tbc ++**.

"U-235, some sort of German U-boat?"

"Possibly, even though the coast line of South America would stretch their operational range. Fissile materials suggest a weapon component or a modified version of the German hollow charge shell. That's the nature of the blueprints and schematics, there, apparently," said Bracken.

"Where did this intelligence come from?" asked de Witte.

His head was tilted slightly, mouth slightly open, his ears fully attuned to every breath and movement in the room.

"Diplomatic pouch from Moscow," replied Gageby.

"From whom?" asked de Witte.

"Stavka headquarters. No name," replied Bracken.

Gageby spread out the documents, each was placed delicately, as he did this he spoke with slow deliberation.

"A U-boat, transporting someone, or something, into or out of South America?"

"We don't know. The PM and the War Office are concerned by this; the Germans have taken a pasting in the East and really should be on the back foot by now. But they're not. This 'uranium machine' reference has appeared almost as an accident among the other intelligence we are here to discuss," said Bracken.

"How has this information come to light may I ask, Mr. Bracken?"

"Through one of my sources, Director. The PM would like Henry Chainbridge to follow up on this 'uranium machine'. I believe Mr. Chainbridge has had some luck disrupting the Abwehr and Gestapo activities recently," said Bracken.

His pomaded thick red hair shone like a sea at sunset.

"Chainbridge is a bit of an odd man out, Minister, he's inclined to follow his own tack," said Gageby.

"When he goes on his own tack, he seems to get results," said Bracken.

"Chainbridge and some of his team are embedded in Germany and they are waiting for further orders. Two of his other operatives,

Brandt and Molenaar, I believe are on assignment in Argentina; translation and decryption work." Said Gageby.

"Miss Molenaar also liquidated a target, I believe, an off-the-books operation?" said Bracken.

"Sanctioned at the highest level." Replied Gageby.

"Indeed. The PM wishes me to take over this team for the foreseeable future, so Miss Molenaar and Captain Brandt will have to be appraised. Chainbridge can liaise with them." said Bracken.

"Minister, with respect, Chainbridge has been gradually building a network through the various peace circles in Berlin and has met with General Ludwig Beck and various parties plotting against Hitler, there is a possibility we can assassinate him." said Gageby.

He clenched and unclenched his fists under the desk; months had been spent setting this up and now it was being taken out of his hands. He tried to supress his disdain for Churchill's closest advisor in the Sedbergh tie.

"The nub of this intelligence is that all it would take to create this level of concern is twenty kilograms of fissile material used as a weapon. It's no longer a national concern, but an Allied concern. Please arrange to have all of Chainbridge's team's dossiers and internal service files transferred to my department immediately. Both officially and unofficially, they now no longer exist," said Bracken.

Before Gageby could respond, de Witte cleared his throat.

"These de-cryptions have come from various sources, gentlemen. There is a common thread here in this country – both Henry Chainbridge and I have followed a number of individuals since 1938. Through our enquiries, the same individual's name keeps appearing – Charles Foucault. I've found his name amongst a number of Lloyds shipping lists, supplied to me recently. I suspect he is using his wealth and influence to ship materials that may be harmful to the allied war effort."

The stone walls gave his voice a slight echo.

Bracken ran his eyes over the intelligence; de-crypted communiqués between numerous agents of the Abwehr and transcribed telephone records and photographs of Foucault in the company of a number of Oswald Mosley's Blackshirts.

"Also, my colleague, Henry Chainbridge, believes the Abwehr have infiltrated the Polish government-in-exile here in London. One of their agents delivered a German radio transceiver to Charles Foucault to his offices in the admiralty. This transceiver, I must stress, is missing."

"This is very compelling, but also highly speculative. Mr. de Witte and director Gageby, what you are suggesting is the unthinkable. I doubt if subjects loyal to the crown and the war effort would be doing this and MI5 have indicated that this simply isn't the case."

Gageby cleared his throt.

"Mr. de Witte here, was captured in New York and held in Abwehr HQ in Berlin. The only people who knew he was in New York were the PM, MI6 and I. Yet, someone managed to expose him."

"And SOE, New York, with respect, director," replied Bracken.

Bracken lit a cigarette, the blue smoke drifted about his immaculately pressed suit.

"How long were you in the Abwehr HQ, Mr. de Witte?"

"Eight, maybe nine weeks."

"Did you suffer?"

"Others there suffered worse. The details are there of my de-brief with SOE."

Gageby interrupted.

"If you're suggesting this is some form of elaborate disinformation…"

"No, director, I am not suggesting anything, but we need to approach this matter delicately. I'll discuss the option of informing the OSS him when I meet the PM at Checkers later today."

"And MI5, MI6?" asked Gageby,

"Keep them appraised. The actions of an eccentric nobleman, however tenuous at the moment, shouldn't affect their work."

Bracken stared directly at de Witte.

"We need, as the Americans say – 'a smoking gun' to prove treachery and treason, no radio transceiver, no espionage performed."

"Of course. Now, am I to assume I'm fit for duty?"

"I've seen your psychiatric assessment. Do you feel ready to return to work?" Bracken replied.

"I do."

"Then please continue."

They watched him rise and leave, each step assured.

"A blind spymaster," murmured Bracken. "Director Gageby, do you think Abwehr Berlin could've turned him?"

Gageby thought for a moment.

"I think he's made of sterner stuff that would have stood him in good stead during his incarceration. There's always the risk, but his knowledge of Russian makes him invaluable. He fought the Bolsheviks in the civil war and it cost him his sight. Truth-be-told, I'd rather him a German agent than a Russian one; at least we know what the Germans are up to."

"They are a hundred miles from the coast and on most nights, directly overhead, D.G." Gageby inwardly baulked at the Irishman's familiarity. "The Russians are waiting for the much-vaunted second front from the allies. We have a considerable work-force in the country working toward this goal, who may well embrace Bolshevism if things get any worse for them. It's my job, D.G., to ensure the right sort of message keeps this from happening."

In the corridor they watched de Witte stride toward the elevators and smartly saluting at the armed marine at the door.

They followed behind in silence. Bracken paused,

"Mr. de Witte will be re-assigned to the Russia desk, not at Bletchley, keep him where he is. Russia is now becoming our priority. Churchill's enamoured with the aristocracy and I doubt he'll sanction spying on the very people he sees as keeping the country going. It's all about the message; chins up and all that."

At the Station's entrance, Driver Knox met de Witte and took his arm to lead him down a step then he walked unaided to the waiting car.

"Miss Knox!" called out Gageby.

Once she had assisted de Witte into the back seat, she came back, saluting smartly.

"Miss Knox, I need to know everything about Mr. De Witte, any changes in behaviour, manners, anything untoward and remember, you signed the official secrets act and therefore, answer directly to me."

"Yes, sir."

She was shaken by the brusque manner of the director, she sensed his dislike of a woman in uniform. Once she sat in the driver's seat, de Witte asked:

"What did the director want?"

"Nothing, sir."

Lies built upon lies thought de Witte. Eva had once described their existence as that.

"Home, Deborah, please."

FOUR
Buenos Aires

Eva Molenaar rolled over and propping herself up on her elbow, watched him as he slept. His body was lean and toned, muscular around the shoulders and tapering down to narrow hips. She watched his chest rise and fall in deep slumber. His body was scarred in places, the nicks and welts of his vocation. He was her mountaineer. Her lover; Brandt. She studied his face, his tight cropped hair, stubble and his eye lashes that had a tint of red. With her rich, lush auburn hair covering him, she listened to his heart, pounding like a locomotive piston under the ribcage. She and Brandt had been working apart for weeks. The Allied Intelligence services were fighting a discreet and dirty little war in the streets below with their German opposites. While across the ocean, a million tragedies were being played out to the sound of falling bombs, exploding shells and whistling bullets. Now they were together again.

Her eyes drifted to the window of the apartment, the world outside going about its business at a Latin pace. Eva touched her belly, imaging the hollow within filled with a tiny heartbeat. Their love-making was always playful, satisfying but careful. Maybe, one day, when it was all over…

She felt Brandt stir and she planted little kisses across his firm gut. Smiling, she took his hardening member and sitting astride him, eased it into her. He murmured, then awoke, grinning.

"Good morning, Brandt…" she said "…this is your wake up call."

Gripping her hips, his own began to push hard, forcing himself deeper into her.

They timed their climax, with the assurance of kindred's, breaking free at the very last moment.

"Now it's time for your English lesson, Brandt…"

He swore under his breath in German.

"Ah," she teased him, "now you owe me breakfast."

His eyes took in her perfect figure and made a playful grab for her. She slipped from his grasp, grinning, and then flicked her hair back. He saw her serious expression; the one you didn't argue with.

"Now, now, fun's over – repeat after me, Brandt..."

***

The Café Moreira in the barrio of San Telmo, was quiet. The bevelled mirrors that spanned the bar reflected the morning sunlight amid the kaleidoscope of tables. The finish of the wooden floor beneath the tables had been smoothed to different shades by the shoes of the nightly tango dancers. Eva studied the room; it was an old style colonial interior, with a radio playing a lush Di Sarli tango that pulsed to the beat of the overhead fans.

Brandt was at the counter talking to the man working there. He paid him a few dollars and joined her.

"Well, it's certainly off the beaten track."

His eyes flicked around the bar, through the wide glass windows he watched a game of chess between two scholarly types. They looked like Russian émigrés, engrossed and scratching their beards as they pondered their moves. Russian was spoken as commonly as Spanish amid the shoppers and tradesmen they had passed to get here.

"Do you play, Brandt?"

"I did, Eva; my father could play four or five games in his head. He was in a room with five paraplegics like himself. I'd visit him every day and they'd be shouting out moves to him, and he'd be shouting out the counter-moves; there was a lot of shouting in that room. Then, he'd drag me into the games, it took a while, but I eventually got the hang of it, shouting out my moves with the lot of them. It was his idea and it kept them all from giving up hope in that infirmary."

With a smile he turned to her.

"Do you?" then nodded at her grin, "…of course you do."

The coffees arrived and Eva asked for a chess board. Throughout the morning, she won two games and lost one. The coffees and food were on Brandt.

"This relationship is starting to cost me," he murmured as he paid the waiter.

"The thing I love about chess, Brandt, is that it always offers possibilities."

A man placed a battered attaché case on the table in front of them.

"Perdone, is this seat taken?"

Eva's Section Chief, Henry Chainbridge eased himself into the chair. He looked careworn, yet meticulously dressed in a light fawn suit, open shirt with a crisp Panama hat tilted jauntily, shading his eyes. He opened his ornate Russian cigarette case, which for once, didn't look at odds with its surroundings.

"Still three a day Nick?"

Brandt nodded and refused the offered cigarette with a smile. Eva took one and she and Chainbridge shared a light from his army lighter.

"I really should cut down, I know." Chainbridge ordered a coffee. He was clearly crumpled from his journey, yet, seemed to stoically accept it.

"This place is very discreet, we can speak freely here," said Brandt.

The man behind the counter raised the volume of the radio.

"Well done, Eva, even his accent is neutral."

She glanced over at Brandt, and stroked his temple once.

"He's a good student, though can be a little temperamental sometimes."

Brandt broke the moment by leaning in towards Chainbridge.

"It must be important if we're meeting face-to-face."

"We have a new Head office; we are now part of Department Int.7. I'm here to advise you of this personally. Int.7 wants us to look in on an individual from London, who's here in Buenos Aires."

From his attaché case he produced a travel guide and slid it over to Eva. Brushing her hair over her ear, she leafed through the pages; Chainbridge was aware of the couple's orbit, the subtle language of lovers.

"Charles Foucault, veterinary pharmaceutical magnate and horse breeder. He has a number of his horses running here over the next few weeks."

Eva found amid the pages a photograph, a black and white shot of an elegant looking man, with the chiselled features of a film star dressed in smart tweeds.

"There are several races at the Hipodromo Argentino de Palermo, mostly charity and in the evenings, benefit balls. As the Argentinean government lean towards Berlin, they're taking an unusual amount of interest in these events. What interests them, interests us. Eva, you and I will be attending the races and evening galas, posing as free-lance journalists. Nick, you're a now Swiss national and we'd like to you to check up on something."

"My pleasure, Henry, what is it?"

"*The Aurora*, a freighter that Foucault shipped his horses on. Undergoing a refit, reason unspecified."

"I'm an engineer, Henry?"

"You're going to get some hands-on experience which we'll discuss once everything has been arranged. We've included some technical details we'd like you to memorise. I'm staying at the Hotel Voltaire in the city, room 101, under the name, Jameson Williams. Best say your farewells this afternoon, your superiors in the monitoring stations have been made aware of your immediate transfer. I'll meet you at nine in the morning. Make separate journeys, and please take extra care with your usual precautions."

"With respect, Henry, how is this helping the early ending of the war?" asked Brandt.

"I'm aware you took an oath to Germany," started Chainbridge.

"Not Hitler, Henry, not him. I am a proud German," replied Brandt.

"I know, Nick, I know, but every small step you make with us, with Eva, myself, every slight set-back or obstacle we create for Hitler and his goons, lessens his grip on power."

"We all have families in Germany, Henry. If the Gestapo get wind, even a hint, we're still alive, then they are all dead," replied Brandt.

"Meenagh's dead," said Chainbridge.

Eva and Brandt sat bolt upright.

"Luftwaffe raid, I'm told. She died instantly, felt nothing" said Chainbridge.

Eva reached out and took his hand. The soft press of flesh amplifed the fact of his loss to him.

"I'm so sorry, Henry,"

"We all have our crosses to bear, Herr Brandt. There are many like you working undercover in the Reich, working towards a free Germany. We'd like you to bring your skills and intelligence to this. You can of course, decline, you've settled your blood debt with your betrayers. You will both of course, be adequately compensated for your efforts."

"And give the devil his due." Said Brandt, "I'll take that cigarette now."

Chainbridge rose and doffed his hat to them.

"Something like that, Nick. Good day."

Brandt sat back and stared at the ceiling. He counted the rotation of the fan blades as another song on the radio broke the silence. He smoked quietly. Eva watched the smoke swirl about him, caught in the fans downdraft.

She leaned in.

"We really should have that dance we promised ourselves, Brandt."

"After the war, we agreed?"

"I want us to have one dance, tonight. We passed a salon down the street, there's a milonga tonight. Next week, Brandt, we'll be in other parts of the world and we may never be here again."

Brandt leaned in and held her face, staring into her grey eyes that sometimes had flecks of green, *like emeralds floating in ice*, Chainbridge had once described them.

"Then we shall dance and tomorrow, we will find out what new adventures Henry has for us."

***

"You know, Brandt, this is considered a very sinful dance."

"Apt then, wouldn't you say, Eva?"

Brandt guided Eva to the floor. She pressed her face to his; their bodies moving to the rhythm of the band, the heat and smells of the room blending with the music. They stared deep into each other's eyes, oblivious to the other couples around them. She could feel the play of his muscles beneath his shirt. He inhaled her hair, her body felt soft and taut at the same time. The hours passed and they found a discreet table and between courses, kisses, coffees, wine and brandy, they danced tango after tango as if it was their last night on earth.

"Thank you for the most perfect evening, Captain Brandt."

"Until tomorrow, Miss Molenaar."

They were professionals again.

FIVE
Buenos Aires

Henry Chainbridge sat staring out of the Hotel Voltaire's window at the Avenida del Liberator. Below the thoroughfare was immense, and yet the morning traffic was still vying for space. He felt cut adrift. In his solitary moments, like tonight, he grieved quietly for his wife, Meenagh. He unfolded the telegram informing him of her death, as neatly creased as the day it was handed to him.

He decided this would be his last mission.

On the ornate desk in the hotel room, were the stacked files from his attaché case, a coffee cup, saucer, a crystal ashtray with a healthy stack of butts, a half-finished bottle of vodka and Webley revolver. He had tried lying on the comfortable bed, but couldn't sleep. He recalled the circuitous journey of nearly thirteen thousand miles to be here, flying out of London after Meenagh's funeral on a chartered Boeing 314 flying boat. On board, was an officious looking man by the name of Curran; whose demeanour was that of a permanently repressed sneer.

"My condolences for your loss, Mr. Chainbridge, but we have very little time. This clipper will rendezvous with the British fleet auxiliary in the South Atlantic for refuelling before arriving in Buenos Aires. Apologies for being so abrupt, but I need get you appraised as quickly as possible, Mr. Bracken was adamant that you get to Argentina by the fastest possible means."

The elusive Brendan Bracken, Churchill's unofficial right-hand man, thought Chainbridge, what was he up to?

"You may not be aware of this, Chainbridge, but Bracken has created a new department: Int. 7. You and your team now come under their remit."

Curran produced a number of manila files and opened them out onto a sliding table for the seat in front of him. In the files were reconnaissance photographs.

"A team of Norwegians were dropped into Telemark to destroy Hitler's heavy water facility, and were successful. Now, Hitler may have gotten his nose bloodied at Stalingrad, but vast amounts of the Soviet Union are still under his control, here."

Curran pointed to a ridge of mountains on one of the high altitude photographs. The notes in white ink were in Russian.

"Urus Martan, taken two months ago. It's a mountain range inside the Soviet Union's borders with good rail link to the Crimean ports. There's heavy excavation work going on at the moment; twenty-four hours, POW and Chinese slave labour courtesy of the Japanese. The whole zone is heavily defended by Waffen SS Wiking Korps under the command of SS-Obergruppenführer Kurt Dietrich Hoeberichts and the Soviets can't get anywhere near them. Alongside it, is an immense industrial complex, we think it's some kind of power plant. The Intelligence here is from among other sources, recently promoted to Commissar, Valery Yvetchenko, you met him in Moscow last year at the conference, I believe."

"I did, a very capable fellow. We co-operated last year with his department in the Stavka. We returned several pieces of priceless Russian art to them and they have given us some several nuggets of intelligence in return."

Chainbridge studied the terrain around the mountain area. It looked like a vast groove, a deep 'V' shape being carved into the rock.

"So you think Germany is building another heavy water plant at Urus Martan?"

"We do. It takes enormous amounts of electricity; and the industrial area suggests they've built one."

"So, why so far away from the Fatherland? It'd make more sense to build one nearer to Berlin or Western Europe?"

"This," Curran produced a dossier stamped **'Eyes-only: Cabinet level'**.

Chainbridge flicked through it, he came to a number of words underlined – fissile materials, Uranium U-235, lithium deuteride, U-233, beryllium.

"We think the Germans are tinkering with Uranium. If they have access to these elements and sieve them all together, in theory we're looking at a very serious threat. Now, Nazi Germany has direct access to Argentinean mining operations and the Japanese are also stripping these materials out of their empire too. They are being delivered into the Crimea rather than through Kiel or Hamburg. That in itself, is unusual."

"Stalin has no problem hurling huge numbers of his troops and aircraft at the Germans without worrying about their losses, why doesn't he send enough force to overwhelm the zone?"

"Because he has his eyes on Western Europe and he knows the tide is slowly turning in his favour. The Reich is running out of time and they and Stalin know it."

Curran produced a file of Lloyds shipping lists, and a copious dossier.

"From your good friend, Peter de Witte: he believes Charles Foucault and numerous members of the English nobility are smuggling these materials into the Crimea under flags of convenience. Foucault has chartered a freighter; *The Aurora*. She was spotted in the Rio de la Plata three days ago. As well as livery, she had a substantial amount of gold bullion and is remaining at anchor there. Martin Bormann has his fingers all over this as *The Aurora* has one of his trusted adjutants on board, Waffen SS Obersturmbannführer Viktor Bausch."

Curran produced a series of photographs, along with Bausch's SS file. Chainbridge glanced down the file – a career Nazi, recent graduate of SS-Junkerschule, highest scores and now private secretary to Bormann.

"Hitler's dream school boy."

"Herr Bausch is trying to redeem himself. Apparently, he's fallen from grace. Bormann has entrusted him with the delivery of the bullion, what we want to know is, what he has bought with it?"

"And you want me and my team to find out if the gold has been used to purchase these fissile materials?"

"Yes, you have two agents in Buenos Aires."

Urus Martan, thought Chainbridge, sounded like one of Dante's rings of hell. He smoked a cigarette as he read, Curran kept adding to the files with notes and observations.

"Ah, now dinner, Henry, I believe its fillet of Sturgeon."

The Flying boat refuelled half-way by the Royal Navy, in relatively calm seas and within two days, Chainbridge and Curran disembarked at a private jetty in Buenos Aires.

At the jetty, two men dressed in the ill-fitting black suits of the Russian secret service, whisked them through to two identical black Zils. They took Chainbridge and Curran in separate directions; Curran to the British Mission, on the outskirts of the city, Chainbridge to the hotel.

The ornate phone on the desk rang,

"A Miss Eileen Sheridan and a Mr. Paul Hauk wish to see you, Mr Williams."

"Please send them up."

He kept his revolver by his side when he opened the door. Eva and Brandt stood outside.

"Welcome." He said.

SIX

Hipodromo Argentino de Palermo, Argentina

The horses stamped and snorted in the track's parade ring, their charges draped in fluttering silk. As the stable hands led them out from the premier enclosure toward the starting gates, each animal twitched, cried and lurched in anticipation of the race. The riders were coiled like springs. The race cards were announced in sporadic bursts from the PA's loudspeakers in Spanish and English.

Eva stood outside Foucault's immense Bedouin-shaped marquee in a cream dress, matching broad hat and comfortable flat shoes, her camera poised and her press card pinned to her lapel. Though independently wealthy, she had opted for stylish, affordable chic. Beside her, in a well-pressed summer suit and dapper trilby stood Henry Chainbridge. Their press passes and Irish Free-State passports were taken from them by a pug-faced security man.

"We'll have these back to you in a jiffy," he said without a smile.

After a beat, an immaculately attired man appeared,

"Welcome Mr Williams, Miss Sheridan, may I introduce myself, I am Cameron Menzies, Lord Foucault's equerry. For your information, Mr. Foucault's horse, Hapsburgh, will be running in The Gran Premio de Honor at the three fifteen, so there's precious little time for an interview. That said, he is very keen to meet you both."

Inside the marquee, long dining tables were set in silver and crystal. Champagne pyramids flowed to laughter and applause. A tango demonstration was in progress.

Past the reception, an area within the marquee was screened off from the guests. Behind it, was a table with five people; four men and a woman looking through leather bound books. On the table were passports, press passes and gilded invitations. Within the leaves of the leather books were lines of photographs of Allied agents. Some had red crosses through them, indicating they were deceased. The woman was tall, voluptuous, sewn into her dress. Her blonde hair was pinned up accentuating her slender neck. She re-read Eva's press pass, identity papers and passport. She held the photograph against the images of known female agents. Once she finished with the living agents, she started again going through the lines of photographs with the red crosses. She came to one that was close, very close. Under the photograph was the name 'Eva Molenaar, Polish national, killed, Oct 1941, Finland.'

It was the same woman.

"Her," she handed the book over to Obersturmbannführer Viktor Bausch. Dressed in a morning suit and white-tie, he gave off the air of a man permanently out of place in civilian life.

"Are you sure?" he said.

Hannah Wolfe nodded.

"Without doubt."

"Who is the man with her then, Wolfe?"

"Possibly British intelligence, he resembles a Swiss expert I met in Italy last year." Said Hannah. She began methodically turning the pages of the male agents. No picture matched.

"I'll let Menzies know." Said Bausch.

Menzies guided Eva and Chainbridge through the crowd after handing back their documentation. He was of medium build with a slight limp, dressed in black jodhpurs and highly polished boots and tweeds that looked better suited to English winters.

Coming face to face with Foucault, Eva was flattered at his appraisal of her; in the flesh, he was deceptively handsome. She had met him once before, at a masked ball in a mansion outside London, in 1937. He was the personification of a time before the war, of cocktails on trans-Atlantic Zeppelins, pleasure cruises and servants at his beck-and-call. He broke from a group of white tie men and their haute couture ladies and shook Eva's hand rather than kiss it.

"Miss Sheridan, and Mr. Williams, freelance journalists, I see. Welcome to my soiree," he swept his arm expansively. On his left hand was a 1926 Rolex oyster watch.

"May I…?" she raised her camera and Foucault grinned into the flash.

"Do you like to gamble, Miss Sheridan?"

"No, I'm afraid not, Mr. Foucualt," Eva replied.

"…and you, Mr. Williams?"

"Occasionally, when I think the odds are in my favour."

"Ahh, an Irish accent, most of my stable hands are from there, inveterate gamblers the lot of them. Do I hear a trace of a Londonderry there?"

Chainbridge remained silent.

Foucault laughed.

"Very good, very good; a man of few words, I like that, like that indeed – now, what is the feature you wish to write?"

"What brings you to Argentina?"

Chainbridge produced his Russian cigarette case. Foucault's eyes turned steely.

"England is bankrupt under Churchill, can't get decent odds or returns anymore. Fascinating little gew-gaw you have there, Williams."

"Thank you." Chainbridge offered a cigarette. "Not Russian, I'm afraid, their tobacco is an acquired taste. This, however, is Turkish."

It was hard to gauge what Foucault despised more; Russians or Turks.

"Thank you, Williams, but no."

He produced his own cigarette case, slim and gold. He accepted a light from Chainbridge. On Foucault's ring finger was a thick, silver ring with what appeared to be a discoloured, misshapen stone fixed into it.

"Interesting little gew-gaw you have there, yourself, Mr. Foucault."

"Thank you, it is a piece of Wat Tyler's jawbone. He was beheaded by an ancestor of mine."

"Thirteen-eighty-one, over taxed, the Southern English counties rose against the crown, led by Tyler. He negotiated terms; the crown reneged on their promises and his head ended up hanging from a bridge over the Thames."

"Excellent summation, Williams, can't have the great unwashed telling us what to do, now can we?" He tipped a wink to Eva.

"I wouldn't take you for a religious man, Foucault," said Chainbridge. Foucault raised an eyebrow.

"You have me at a loss."

"Wearing an old relic."

"Ah, yes, well it had been handed down through my family from generation to generation, a constant reminder of what's correct and proper."

Foucault,'s eyes never left Eva and during the interview, he smoothly evaded Chainbridge's question of how the horses travelled to Argentina. He was curt when asked about three German horses racing in his silks; two belonged to Hermann Goering.

Her attention turned to the other guests and she raised her Lecia for a group shot. A cluster of men in ill-fitting though expensive business suits were watching from a reserved table. One of the men was an imposing presence, like the old priest of her childhood,

Grabowski, who would stare from the pulpit in her home town like a zealous crow. The imposing man, held a large leather-bound book; a bible and drank iced tea with his free hand. He refrained from conversation. Standing beside the reserved table were several American naval personnel in white, crisp uniforms. The band switched to a merengue and couples took to the floor to dance.

A tall, handsome American naval officer asked her to dance.

"Sorry, I'm on duty," she jerked a thumb back at Chainbridge.

"Join us for a drink at least," he said. He was fresh faced, tall and groomed, but he wasn't Brandt.

"Just one, then."

She could feel Foucault's stare boring into her.

Deflecting the officer's clumsy, folksy, apple-pie, advances, she overheard a junior officer over her shoulder say,

"We're returning to dry dock – the old man's getting a bath fitted, can't use the showers."

Overhearing this, the group of ill-suited men laughed.

"Sad old cripple," said the Bible-man with unexpected resonance, "Dying too, I hear. Stalin will miss his ass-kissing…" he wheezed a laugh into the glass at his own joke.

Chainbridge had heard it too. He had seen a warship in the bay. It had resembled a fortress.

It was Franklin D. Roosevelt's flagship.

The public address system blared out a bugle blast for the next race.

"Ah, the 2.30's about to start, we're on after that. Please join me at my private box in the Grandstand," said Foucault.

Raising a hand, he gestured for a man holding a silver plate at the marquee entrance who made his way through the dancers on the floor. Foucault placed a chit on the silver plate.

"Santiago, on the nose for the 3.15, best possible odds."

Eva leaned in, allowing him to catch her scent.

"Not Hapsburgh then?"

"God no, Eileen, he's the favourite. The stable lads tell me Santiago's about to peak and they are always spot on with their tips."

Eva produced from her purse a US hundred-dollar bill.

"Best odds on Santiago too, please," she held Foucault's steady gaze.

"Freelance photography pays well these days, I see, Eileen."

"I'm a woman of means, Mr. Foucault."

"Charles, call me Charles."

"Charles, then."

He spied the handsome Officer hovering, trying to catch her eye.

"Eileen, do you like Opera?"

Chainbridge interrupted.

"Thank you for the interview. I'll file this to the offices in London."

"May I keep this delightful creature with me for the afternoon?"

Chainbridge smiled.

"Miss Sheridan is very much her own woman, I'm just an associate."

Eva turned to Foucault.

"I'd love to, Charles."

"Excellent, I'll introduce you to some friends and the mighty Hapsburg," he offered her his arm.

Chainbridge touched Eva's shoulder.

"I'll take your camera, Eileen, and will have the photographs forwarded on. Thank you again, Mr. Foucault."

The men shook hands; the faint whiff of sulphur came off the two of them.

"Good afternoon, Williams."

"Foucault."

The private box gave a clear view of the track high above the Tattersall. A sea of people in their finery, shouted, cried and cheered as their wagers turned on the inside straight. In the fan cooled room, Eva was offered chilled champagne and binoculars by Foucault.

The ten horses tore around the track urged on by the crowds. Santiago, the black stallion, churned the soil beneath its deceptively slender legs as he broke free of the field. Almost as soon as it started, the race was over.

Santiago had won by two lengths. Foucault, used to screaming girls, noted how cool Eva was.

"Thank you for the tip, Charles."

"Thank you for trusting my judgement, Eileen."

Chainbridge watched them through binoculars. Eva held court amid the Americans and the naval officers. She said something that made them all roar with laughter and another toast was raised.

"Do you think your agent will be ok?" asked Curran who had moved from green to a smart sports jacket and pale slacks. His gaunt features were eclipsed by the brim of his Panama hat.

"Yes, she's well able to look after herself. Here's the camera, she got a good few shots of some American big wigs."

"I'll get it processed immediately. And Brandt?"

"On his way to the Docks. Why is there an American warship here?"

"USS Iowa, Roosevelt's ship. She's about to undergo a refit for the next conference. The big three have a vision of a post-war Germany."

"Germany has to be defeated first, Curran. Best split up, we're being watched, too." Peeking from beneath their hat brims they saw Menzies standing in the private box, watching them through binoculars.

Chainbridge, produced his notebook, with a pencil sharpened at both ends and strode purposely to the winners' enclosure.

He looked back, Eva was now just a cream blur behind the glass.

SEVEN

Buenos Aires

Brandt stared down at the oily waters slopping around the hull of the vessel.

"Ever been on a ship before?" asked Carrington. Chainbridge had introduced him in the hotel; a New Zealander. He was a tall man, if he jumped down onto the deck, he'd still be making eye-contact with me, thought Brandt.

"A dinghy for an hour, but that's it," replied Brandt.

It had been off the coast of Finland and he had been trying to prevent Lenin's body leaving the Soviet Union. That was three years ago; the year he met Eva.

"Suffer from sea sickness?" asked Carrington.

"I didn't then," replied Brandt.

"Trust me, you will," said Carrington. "Can you swim?"

"Yes," replied Brandt.

"Well that's a plus - this is your home for the next week," said Carrington.

He threw his duffel bag onto the uneven deck. A small, burly man appeared from the dilapidated bridge, his unkempt hair was pulled casually across his bald pate, a few strands caught the breeze,

"And this man is going to train you. Pryce, this is Paul Hauk," said Carrington.

"Carrington," nodded Pryce, "what have we got here, then?"

"An oiler," said Carrington.

"A greaser?" replied Pryce. He spat a long stream of tobacco juice onto the deck.

"Exactly," replied Carrington.

Dawn was breaking and Carrington's eyes sought the shadows. He squatted down, lowering his profile.

"Throw down your bag, Mr. Hauk, quickly now."

Brandt tossed the bag, Pryce stepped nimbly out of the bridge and caught it easily. He held it up as he shook it.

"Overalls?"

"In the bag."

Pryce tilted his head at Brandt's voice and his eyes took on a steely glint.

"German?" he asked.

"Swiss," replied Brandt

"Same thing to me," said Pryce.

"You?" asked Brandt

"Not important," replied Pryce.

"Best get aboard, Mr. Hauk," said Carrington.

The eased their way onto the slowly pitching deck.

Ships began to ply their way out of the harbour; the little ship bobbed in their wake.

Brandt offered his hand.

"Hauk. Good to meet you."

"*Nice to meet you.* Sounds more English," whispered Carrington.

Pryce took both of Brandt's hands, his grip intense.

"Good hands, strong hands," he said, turning Brandt's hands over. "Factory worker?"

"Mountaineer," replied Brandt. Pryce's grip intensified.

"Mountaineer?" he said.

"Guide, the odd rescue," replied Brandt.

With a flick of the wrists, he released his hands and grasped Pryce's, matching pressure for pressure.

"Finished reading my palms, Madame Zelda?" he asked.

The glint re-appeared in Pryce's eyes as Brandt's grip tightened.

"For now," replied Pryce. "Know anything about engines?"

"I can start one with a hammer," replied Brandt; it was a common occurrence along the Russian front.

"He'll do," grinned Pryce.

"Now let's show you your new home," said Carrington. "I hope you like enclosed spaces."

He descended into the engine room.

"Jesus Christ," muttered Brandt. It smelled worse than the decks above.

"Let's get to work," said Pryce. The narrow walkway on which they stood sat between two engines.

"Six hours on, six hours off, your bunk is in the bow. Your primary duty is to keep the engines lubricated and familiarise yourself with the gauges," said Carrington.

Brandt wriggled into his overalls.

Pryce studied him momentarily before continuing.

"Think of this humble little vessel as a floating city, it needs light, water, electricity and sanitation."

"Sanitation?" asked Brandt.

"Toilets fall under the remit of the oiler, boyo. Now let's begin with the engines," said Pryce.

Brandt pulled the folded engine schematics Chainbridge had given to him from his pocket. Pryce snatched them out of his hands and crumpled them.

"You pull these out on The *Aurora*, you are exposed and we are all dead," said Pryce.

Brandt stepped forward until he was toe-to-toe with the diminutive man. Pryce didn't budge an inch.

"This isn't the *Aurora* and I'm a thorough man, Pryce," said Brandt.

"He's right, Mr. Hauk. No papers, just hands-on," said Carrington. He was stooping so low; he was almost addressing the floor.

"The docks have eyes and ears everywhere, Mr. Hauk – by now we've been seen and noted, we will have been remarked on in the wharf side taverns and yes, we may even reach the ears of Mr.

Foucault and his low-life comrades in the Abwehr by nightfall," said Pryce, his steely gaze switched over Brandt's shoulder.

"Best get underway, Mr. Carrington, also radio Chainbridge, let him know his esteemed colleague is safely aboard."

"Now, Mr. Pryce. Show me what to do," said Brandt.

Pryce produced two thick wads of cotton wool and divided them up into four.

"For your ears," he said, stuffing two wads into his own.

The engines belched into life and the little boat glided out into the River Plate and out toward the ocean.

***

A few hours later, in the galley, Brandt worked a rag through his fingers. A purple lump under his thumbnail throbbed dully; a spanner had slipped.

Carrington slid a piece of grilled fish onto his plate. Pryce was piloting the boat into the waves. The ship pitched and swayed.

"You use your senses, Mr. Hauk," he shouted as the ship tilted wildly downwards, "anything untoward you spot, feel or see you report to the chief engineer."

"I can't understand a word he's saying," said Brandt.

His head was throbbing from the relentless pulsing engines.

Carrington looked over from the small grill.

"He's Welsh, I struggle myself, Hauk." he replied.

Brandt felt ill and the fish slid up his throat as quickly as it went down.

He dashed to side of the boat and vomited into the ocean.

"Fuck you, Chainbridge," he muttered.

The sea flowed past and poured in over the gunwale and swept along the decks. Brandt eyed the big volumes of water trying to flow out through the scuppers from the vessel's deck with unease.

He could still hear Pryce intoning out the meanings of each gauge from within the bridge as if he was still sitting there.

It was going to be a long, long week thought Brandt.

He vomited spittle and coffee and that was all that was left inside.

He had another six hour shift ahead and he dry retched at the prospect.

***

"That's an interesting tattoo," said Carrington.

It was three days into the voyage, and both men were stripped to the waist, the heat of the engine room was oppressive.

"It's a shark," replied Brandt.

"Pretty cut up," said Carrington.

"Climbing accident," replied Brandt.

"With a bayonet? I've seen injuries like that." Carrington's voice, despite sounding neutral, had an undertow of menace. Cooped up for hours on end had brought an edge to their conversations.

"A piton came loose," said Brandt.

Carrington studied Brandt for a moment, then climbed up on deck.

"With a man on the other end of it," he said over his shoulder.

Brandt made a mental note to have the tattoo removed.

Eva had hated it, the scarred ink; the wound had been inflicted by a Polish soldier during the German invasion in 1939, a solitary little skirmish in the mountains; an even hand-to-hand fight with only one winner.

Brandt's confidence had grown since this morning, the engines had offered a few challenges and both Pryce and Carrington had left him to figure out the problems that did arise. Now both engines were running smoothly.

Suddenly, without warning, they slowed down and came to a stop.

Pryce's head appeared above him.

"Come have a look at this, Mr. Hauk."

The little vessel dropped anchor and the three men fed out shipping nets. Pryce then went to the bridge and began sending a coded message.

A few miles off the bow, was an enormous luxury liner.

"There she is, bang on time - that's the *Serenity*," said Carrington.

Brandt looked at it through the binoculars handed to him.

"So?" he asked.

"Look just ahead of her bows, after the next wave."

The little vessel pitched and for a moment two thin glittering periscopes left narrow wakes ahead of *Serenity*'s bow.

"Focault's private yacht with a U-boat escort," said Carrington.

"U-boat? U-235, maybe?" asked Brandt.

"Too low in the water to see any livery," replied Carrington.

"If we can see them, then they can see us," muttered Brandt. His stomach twisted in fear; a single torpedo could blow them to kingdom come.

"This is a busy shipping lane. They'll leave us be." said Carrington.

Pryce appeared at the bridge.

"*Serenity* – Foucault's private yacht – she's a Blohm und Voss luxury vessel, four hundred feet long with a complement of forty-four crew. Inside, she's all Italian marble, best champagne cellar, gold-plated faucets and barstools upholstered with whale's foreskins – if you believe his pronouncements to all and sundry. She's a fast little number. I've alerted Buneos Aires station; they're sending decrypts to London."

"Send on *U-boat contact*, tag *U-235* too," said Brandt.

"Best act like fishermen, gentlemen," said Carrington.

They donned heavy work jackets and thick woollen hats.

The luxury yacht sailed on.

"I think you're ready to be the oiler on *The Aurora*," said Pryce.

"How do you figure that?" replied Brandt.

"Because I'm the Bosu'n, Mr. Hauk and I'll be signing you on myself. Both vessels will be leaving Buenos Aires the day after tomorrow."

They waited until nightfall and hauled in the nets.

Brandt collapsed into his bunk and fell asleep, no longer aware of the tossing of the vessel.

They were heading back to Buenos Aires.

EIGHT

100km west of Buenos Aires

Viktor Bausch had decided at this point that he hated Americans. Endless talk, always about money, and god. God. From the race course they had flown in Foucault's private C-69 aircraft to the landing strip camouflaged on either side by dense woodland. Bormann's immense private JU390 was being refuelled as they landed. Bausch stepped down along with the others and marvelled at the smooth asphalt airstrip and the immense four-engine aircraft. Both were impressive feats of engineering, hacked out of the sylvan shade. The rumours were true, he thought; Bormann was getting ready to run for it. The Englishman, Foucault, though was another matter.

"Welcome gentlemen to my little bolt-hole," he'd grinned.

"A German bomber?" one of the Americans had asked. It dwarfed Foucault's airliner.

"She's a proto-type, long range bomber, can reach New York without re-fuelling, so the boffins tell me. This isn't the United States of America by the way, this is Argentina," said Foucault.

They stood in a line as the engines belched into life.

"Herr Bormann has set this site up without the high command's knowledge. I'm naturally happy to help out where possible," said Foucault tipping his panama lower over his eyes.

The JU390 seemed incapable of leaving the ground but with a final roar, it ascended and banked skyward like an injured condor.

"It'll be in Berlin by midnight tomorrow," said Foucault.

Through a pathway, they saw the huge aircraft hangars covered in camouflage netting. Anti-aircraft crews idled over magazines, coffee and cigarettes. They glanced up at the party and then returned to their preoccupations.

Past the forest cover they made their way across manicured lawns and croquet hoops.

"Home sweet home, gentlemen; my private stud; my converted estancias, *Casa Rosa,*" said Foucault.

Divided into pairs, swapping partners, they had been playing for several hours now. The games room was the only one where the listening devices carefully planted by MI6 and OSS could be disrupted. Foucault was no fool. Bausch chalked his cue with slow clock-wise twists as Foucault broke first. The balls clattered across the smoothed baize in tight clusters. The lavish and dimly lit billiards room was situated in Casa Rosa's upper suites.

Watching the game in the shadows was the American Senator Cooper Clavelle Thurmond and a Japanese officer of the Imperial navy whose name was Nagasawa. Both were attired for the humidity. Thurmond was a clumsy player, Nagasawa was sleek.

Nodding to the Japanese the Senator eased himself into one of the comfortable red leather settees. His frame was corpulent, his buzz-cut hair style giving his head a tapered appearance. His eyes, though, were like Hitler's, thought Bausch – cold, unflinching blue. The senator placed thick horn-rimmed glasses on as he selected a passage from a leather-bound bible that was never far from reach.

"Reichskommisariat Kaukaus will receive the shipment ahead of schedule, thanks to you senator and you, Mr. Bausch," said Foucualt.

"I have ensured Abwehr Buenos Aires have the proposed target co-ordinates. It will be an event that will be heard around the world," said Bausch.

He had cabled his report earlier that day to *Wolfsschanze* in Rastenburg, eyes-only for the Führer, that the project was ahead of schedule. This place reminded him of Rastenburg – mosquitoes, flies and cloying heat.

"A veritable seismic event. Please send our sincere thanks to Reichsleiter Bormann for expediting the bullion, Viktor," said Foucault. He mis-cued, sending the cue ball spiralling. He hissed through his teeth and stabbed the herringbone floor with the butt of the cue.

Bausch moved into the light.

"I will convey it, personally, Herr Foucault," replied Bausch

A day away from Reichsleiter Martin Bormann and the Führer, was a day wasted, he thought. He loved the monologues that drifted into the early hours, the huge map of Russia pinned to the dining room wall where Hitler pointed to the German advance. Stalingrad was never mentioned.

Menzies knocked discreetly and entered. On silver tray, was a decanter of Brandy, balloon-glasses and a box of Cuban cigars. Foucault nodded with a grin; Menzies was a dab hand with a cut-throat razor and had fled England after a fight at Lewes race course. Cheques were written, judges bribed and the victim, quietly buried.

"Thank you, Menzies."

"Anything else before I retire, gentlemen?" asked Menzies.

The Senator didn't look up.

"I never drink, thank you, never drink alcohol. Before I left for Argentina, I fasted for forty-eight hours, god came to me in a vision – I heard his message, I'm still satiated on the love of god; the cripple is the slave of the red, atheist beast, we must act and act soon."

Nagasawa ignored him. Striding to the table, the Japanese poured for three and lit up a cigar in hurried puffs.

"That will be all, Menzies, thank you," said Foucualt, studying Bausch's game.

"Very good, sir."

He marched out of the room.

"We may have a problem," said Bausch. He potted a ball into the far pocket with a flourish.

"Miss Sheridan?"

"Yes."

Bausch mis-shot. He stood up and ground the chalk into the cue. Foucault gave his most charming of smiles,

"Her professional credentials are impeccable; I have made my own enquiries."

"Miss Wolfe, is certain that Sheridan is an Allied agent. She found her in Italy."

"Ah, yes, a fine little doxy, that Miss Wolfe. Just a tad paranoid though."

Foucault began to tidy up the remaining balls on the table.

"Why did that delicious voluptuary decide to remain in Buenos Aires?" asked Thurmond. He licked his thin lips slowly. He dabbed some drool away with his pocket silk handkerchief.

"Keeping tabs on Miss Sheridan. We'll deal with the troublesome journalist after the Opera, just to make certain. We'll throw her a bone and see where the little bitch runs back to; see if she's working for M16."

He finished the game and handed the cue to Nagasawa. Bausch gulped down the brandy and began setting the table for another game. He tried to be as quiet as possible, maybe the Abwehr might be able to piece together the events tonight.

"Will we make this a little more interesting?" Bausch produced a thick wad of dollars; he too had had a successful day at the track. Nagasawa's expression remained neutral.

"Yes."

"The Axis playing each other for the highest stakes, what do you make of that, Senator?" grinned Foucault,

"The Axis are the last bastion against Bolshevism," intoned Thurmond.

"And America, England, Senator?" Replied Foucault.

Thurmond was thumbing his bible, he didn't respond.

After a coin-toss, Nagasawa broke first, stabbing the cue from the shoulder. The resounding crack of the scattered balls rang around the room.

It was clear that from the outset, Nagasawa was going to win. There would be no loss of face tonight.

Foucault lit a cigar and sat beside The Senator. In sotto voice said:

"Have you spoken to our dear friend Michelet?"

"Yes, poor Guy got burned at the races today, he's a very unhappy chappie. He practically put the bloody deeds to the chateau on Hapsburg. Still, he's a true Thule disciple of Himmler's and loyal subject of the Reich. His losses ensure I now have his undivided attention."

"Gambling is the work of the devil, sir. The devil. But we need the sinners as well as the saints for the work that lies ahead of us, Foucault."

His stare was that of a messiah, magnified through the glasses. He emphasised each word with a stab of the finger on the bible's soft leather cover. For a pious man, he had won a small fortune on

Foucault's horses; it had been 'Praise Jesus' all the way when he collected his winnings. He didn't drink alcohol; and for that, Foucault loathed him.

"Senator, you have my word, that deliverance is coming. The way the war is going, we are more likely to see Russian paratroopers gliding over London, rather than the Luftwaffe. If they establish a foothold in England, then America will fall."

He glanced over at Bausch to see if he had been overheard. The game consumed the German's concentration. Coils of veins danced around his shaved skull as the game was clearly slipping from his grasp.

"That day must never come. Never. Tidy up the loose ends. And ensure, sir, that dandy of a Frenchie is prepared," Said Thurmond, his voice had become a deep growl.

Foucault wondered if Senator Cooper Clavelle Thurmond understood the size of this gamble. The plundered Nazi bullion in Vichy-controlled Senegal arranged by Michelet had been sunk into this project. An immense weapon was being assembled inside mountain thousands of miles behind the Russian frontline at the site Urus Martan. The Skoda works in Czechoslovakia had manufactured and delivered a gargantuan breech that would recoil on a mile of rails carved into the mountain's base. With the war practically lost and no country willing to deal with Hitler, it was now down to the fanatics to pull something out of the hat. And there seemed to be no shortage of them at this moment in time.

Maybe Bormann was right – *cut your losses and run.*

Nagasawa roared in triumph as he slotted home a tricky shot. His movements were brisk and fluid to Bausch's steady, plodding deliberation.

They sat back to watch the game.

There was another knock at the door. Foucault looked at his Rolex.

"Gentlemen, the girls have arrived. Local, I'm afraid, but very…welcoming."

He would deal with the loose ends in the morning.

NINE
Moscow

Colonel Marko Kravchenko had the farmer to thank. In the depths of the blizzard, his steppe pony, a small, doe-eyed mare had plodded through the powdery snowdrifts and somehow made her way to the small, isolated farmhouse. Her determined snorts and whinnies had brought the elderly man out from the comfort of his hearth. Kravchenko's heavy coat had frozen solid and the farmer had to push him backward and forward to release him from the saddle. The pony's tough hide and shaggy mane were festooned with icicles.

"Enter!" the farmer had shouted in the howling gale.

Kravchenko was happy to hear spoken Russian again. The farmer, clutching a lantern in one hand, guided the small pony to one of the outhouses that were almost completely buried under the drifts. Kravchenko entered the peasant's hut. It was a modest abode and an elderly woman beckoned him toward the warm hearth. Her demeanour altered slightly when he removed his great coat and she saw first the ragged NKVD uniform and then, the extent of his injuries. The farmer had returned, muttering and cursing under his breath and forced the door closed. The storm responded by sending bitter flurries down the chimney.

Kravchenko had burns to his left arm, the back of his left leg up to the buttock. His beard had been singed on the left side too and he was covered in untreated cuts and lacerations.

The farmer and his wife cleaned him as best they could, stripped his uniform down, and although illiterate, understood the nature of his identity papers.

"Thank you, Comrades," was all he said before falling asleep, sitting upright in the chair.

He slept for a day and woke in a small cot in the corner of the hut. When he propped himself gingerly up, he found his wounds crudely dressed and the farmer's wife offering him a small bowl of borscht. Later that day, the village elders met and arranged Kravchenko's journey out of the Ukraine with local partisans. As the NKVD, were despised by both sides of the Great patriotic war, this was no mean feat. Smuggled through German occupied Ukraine on a mule, Kravchenko managed to reach Moscow by rail; sleeping rough in freezing shunting yards and cowering with terrified conscripts and civilians when the carriages were strafed by the Luftwaffe.

That was four months ago.

Now he stood before his superior, Valery Yvetchenko, at the underground Stavka HQ, Moscow, having been released from convalescence. Yvetchenko was methodical, running a pencil along the lines of Kravchenko's report.

"Welcome back, Comrade, Colonel."

"Congratulations on your promotion, Comrade Commissar 2nd rank of the Soviet Supreme General Staff," said Kravchenko.

"This report is thorough, it was unfortunate to lose a VDV parachute detachment in Romania and you were lucky to escape by the skin of your teeth. If it hadn't been a secret operation, you'd be receiving the order of Lenin at this very minute."

"I'll take that statement, Comrade Commissar Yvetchenko, as honour enough."

Yvetchenko stared over his wire-frame glasses. Kravchenko's clean-shaven face carried faint burn scars, his red hair had grown back and was now tightly cropped. His nose was askew from numerous breaks and re-sets and he carried the air of a worn-out cavalry horse. His eyes though, were now cold and calculating. The Soviet system had moulded him, broken him, remoulded him and he now stood before Yvetchenko, the perfect Bolshevik soldier. He was brave and loyal despite the miseries heaped on him and over the years. Yvetchenko had grown to admire his stoicism.

"I've read your medical report, Comrade Kravchenko, the extent of your injuries sustained in action, mean you are invalided. But as it's all shoulders-to-the-wheel in our great patriotic war with the Germans, you are to be re-assigned."

To some far-flung hell-hole, thought Kravchenko. He was still in pain and longed for the luxury to grieve after all he had been through in the last two years.

"To serve Mother Russia and the party is a sacred duty," he said.

"You and I will be flying to Tehran, Persia and will be liaising with the USSR Assistant Commissioner for foreign affairs, Comrade Vyshinski."

Yvetchenko motioned for Kravchenko to sit. Kravchenko looked around the open canvas sheeted office and spied the legs of a chair under a heap of uniforms and coats.

"Just throw them on the floor."

Yvetchenko handed Kravchenko a series of decryptions and photographs. One was of the blast site where Yvetchenko had met Plutenko.

"I visited here several months ago. Through my enquiries, most of what you see used to be woodland. The Germans seem to have managed to create a bomb, flying rocket or artillery shell that can do this."

Kravchenko studied the decrypted telegram *'Oslo/Tokyo-copper head exceeded expectations and will completely upset all ordinary precepts of warfare hitherto established.'*

"You and I will stay at the Soviet mission in Tehran which is directly behind the British mission where our fellow allies will meet us. They intercepted that message and are chasing down this threat, they think it's a credible one."

"Which means the next allied conference is in Tehran?"

"Yes, Comrade Colonel. We propose that Roosevelt stay at the soviet mission, we'll build a story about Nazi assassins parachuting in and fuel the American's paranoia. You will ensure that all the correct bugging equipment is installed and working perfectly."

Kravchenko looked up into the wrestler's face of Yvetchenko, his skin, under the subway lighting looked waxen, lifeless. His eyes were hidden in the glasses' reflection of his desk lamp.

"It's a death sentence, Commissar," he said.

"I am aware of that, thank you, Comrade Colonel Kravchenko."

"How long have we got to prepare?"

"Not long Comrade Colonel, it's going to be a very high level delegation going to Tehran; Molotov, Beria along with Stalin. We will have three thousand NKVD troops there; the Americans have only a minimal amount of troops along with the British. Roosevelt will be travelling six thousand kilometres by sea, the poor bastard."

"Churchill?"

"By sea too."

Kravchenko rose, his wounds still smarting. He hadn't any living family left, no-one to say goodbye to.

"I shall depart to Tehran, straight away, Comrade Commissar."

Yvetchenko returned to his stack of correspondence and saluted idly.

"Dismissed, Comrade Colonel."

TEN

Buenos Aires

Brandt took the late-afternoon bus from his apartment to a sprawling shanty town for migrant workers near the port. He found the tumbledown shack along a dark and fetid alley where Carrington, would be waiting. At the doorway Brandt knocked in code. Carrington, dressed in an oil-stained vest, corduroy work pants and heavy boots, invited him in. The room was lit with a Davy Lamp. He handed Brandt a Rolliflex camera, a creased boiler suit and metal tool box.

"The dry dock you're looking for is numbered 12. There's a distinctive archway; ornate, white-wash lintel, with the numbers in black Roman numerals. The *Aurora* is undergoing a re-fit there. How's your Spanish?"

"Non-existent."

"Shouldn't present a problem, the place is crawling with Germans. Gun?"

Brandt produced his Mauser. He pulled on the boiler suit. Unlike the one he wore on the fishing boat, it was for a much larger man and allowed a good degree of freedom of movement. He placed the camera at the bottom of the tool box. From inside the box's fold-out drawers, he retrieved a map of the docklands area, official

Argentinian travel permits and union card. In another drawer, a packet of cigarettes, an envelope full of US dollars and glossy playing cards with risqué images. He held the playing cards up with a raised eyebrow; the lanky New Zealander shrugged.

"Ship yard currency."

Brandt nodded and stowed them with the cigarettes and union card on the inside the work clothes.

"Any idea what I'm looking for?"

" 'fraid not, old chum, something out of the ordinary. But be careful."

"I will. Security?"

"Mainly local port police along the quays, but as I said, dry dock #12 is crawling with Germans."

Carrington threw him a weather-beaten peaked cap,

"There's a café bar a mile east along the Quays called *'Los Ingleses'*. Leave the tool box there behind the bar. Ask for the barman; his name is Kelly."

"Have you a knife? Something big?"

Carrington fished around in his own kit bag and produced a big hunting knife in a leather sheath. Brandt pulled the knife and held it up; it glittered in the room's lamp light. It had a serrated cutting edge, polished wooden handle, the butt was a dark metal as was the bolster, and tapered to an effective point. Holding it in the flat of his palm, Brandt admired the weapon's balance.

"Sometimes gun fire draws attention."

"Keep it."

Carrington left the shack with his kit bag over his shoulder, masking his features. Waiting five minutes, Brandt extinguished the lamp and pulling the cap down low over his eyes, stepped out into the night.

He found dry dock #12. Acetylene torches flashed and sparked amid the shouts, whistles and cat-calls of the graveyard shifts. The dock's reception office was small. The two men working there were young, lean and fit, uniformly dressed in open neck khaki shirts. Not slovenly guards working out a sinecure, he thought. They eyed Brandt suspiciously, re-checking his permit and documentation.

"Paul Hauk, unrated oiler, what is the nature of your work?"

"Engineering; some problem with the number two diesel in the engine room," his eyes, shaded by the cap's peak, took in the German-made MP28 machine pistol resting against the desk. His documents were handed back coldly.

"Report to the duty foreman, Remy Schlatter, he's over in the main factory."

The *Aurora*'s immense prow hung in the air from her blocks. Gantries, winches and chains hung from her russet sides. The keel was screened off by high tarpaulin walls. Brandt, looking around, fished out the camera from the box and clicked the shutter several times from hip height. As he started to walk along the walls, looking for a tear or gap in the material, he came upon rows of black tubes, the length of railway carriages. They were knee high and laid out end-to-end, the length of the ship. He counted twenty-eight of them, laid out fourteen each side of the boat. Stopping a passing workman to light a cigarette, he took in the work around him; on the far side of the dock was an industrial estate with men moving around it. Other buildings were also lit up. Looking back at the office with the two guards, Brandt noticed the tall radio aerial antenna coming out of the roof.

"Schlatter?"

The man spat on the ground and jerked a thumb toward the factory. On the other side of the ship and brightly lit by the building's lights, were the same long black tubes. Near the aft section of the vessel, a large crane slowly hoisted up one of the tubes. Shouts and whistles from the men beneath it indicated there was a problem. The tube swung unevenly over the top of the tarpaulins, striking the ship's hull loudly. A small section of the tube fragmented and several pieces of it fell onto the dock. More whistles, shouts and waving told the crane driver to stop and bring the tube back down. It was lowered gingerly and a huddle of foremen and workers formed around the tube. Brandt walked up to the edge of the group and peered in. Curses and oaths were spat out and the general air of unease pervaded the group of men.

"Nothing we can do about it boys; we'll have to do this bloody one again from scratch. One bloody crack could be a problem - someone give that clown in the crane a kicking," muttered one of the foremen in German.

Brandt helped the men heave the tube over towards the factory. It took a gang of twenty men to haul it across the dock. Before the large doors closed, Brandt thought he saw a group of oriental men in naval uniform: Japanese Imperial officers. They were standing beside what looked like a huge smelter, talking to more men dressed like the two in the office. He went back to the tool box he'd left beside the tarpaulin wall; underneath it was a piece of the broken tubing. He placed the fragment inside his boiler suit.

He felt a hand on his shoulder. Spinning around, he came face-to-face with Pryce. His face was oily and it glistened all over his grin,

"Best get to work, Mr. Hauk," said Pryce.

They ascended the gangplank to the engine room.

Though the engines were immense, Brandt recognised the similarity in design to the small boat. Unsupervised, he set about his oiling tasks, from a back pocket in his trousers, he produced a small, creased notebook and pencil and jotted down the readings off the gauges.

Pryce held open a pocket watch, timing him,

"You must work faster, Hauk. The chief engineer is many things, but stupid, he is not."

"Any idea why the keel is screened off?" asked Brandt.

"All very hush, hush, I'm afraid – Foucault's making all of the decisions, something to do with the ship's ballast," replied Pryce.

"Ballast?"

"Some modifications for the voyage out."

Pryce bit off a wad of tobacco.

"Where's the chief engineer?" asked Brandt.

"Off requisitioning every solitary grape in Argentina, I'd imagine," replied Pryce.

Brandt spent twenty minutes working at his own pace, ignoring Pryce's comments, jibes and snide cat-calls. Every calculated movement made by Brandt was designed to antagonise the Welshman further.

Satisfied, Brandt wiped his hands and stowed his equipment. Pryce checked everything, his only communication; tuts and the occasional grunt.

"Very thorough, Mr. Hauk; we might just make a passible greaser of you yet.' He said.

"I'll see you soon, Pryce," replied Brandt.

"A couple of days, modifications aren't going to plan at the moment. I'll send you a message." replied Pryce.

He watched Brandt ascend to the decks and spat a long stream of tobacco juice onto the floor.

Brandt walked across the dock back to the office where the two guards sat.

"What was the commotion out there?" asked one of them.

"The crane driver dropped something," replied Brandt.

"Fools, those Argentinians," said the other one, absently scratching himself. "If this were Hamburg, that bloody crane operator would be on a one-way ticket to the Eastern front by now."

"I just cleaned out the latrines on *The Aurora*, I'd have made them do it," said Brandt.

All three laughed.

Brandt produced the cigarettes.

"These fell out of the thing that was dropped."

It was a packet of Lucky Strikes.

"Bloody hell," said the first one; he looked like he'd been pulling double-shifts, red rimmed eyes above his five o'clock shadow. "Smuggling good stuff to Marseilles?"

Brandt opened the pack and lit three cigarettes.

"... and better yet, these," he produced the playing cards. The cards had photographs of women in various poses, in various stages of undress.

The second one whistled. Brandt noticed he had gone bald early and had delicately pomaded his hair forward to disguise it.

"Definitely Berlin girls, not like the Bavarian country cows, or Polish dogs," he fanned out the cards, and grinned. "Lucky Strikes and pretty little girls. No wonder the whole thing is hush-hush."

"See there's Jap navy here too."

"Place is full of them. Been here for a week and act like they own the place."

Brandt finished his cigarette,

"Hitting they hay gents. Enjoy!" said Brandt. He gave the room a final glance and spied a German army radio on the floor behind the men.

A huge roar of laughter came from the office as Brandt walked out onto the street towards the *Los Ingleses* café bar. From the distance, he could have been any worker heading home from a long shift. He walked not too fast and not too slow, nodding to the odd worker who made eye contact on the street. Across the bay of *La Plata*, the dawn began to break over the smoke stacks and rigging of the ships at anchor, glinting off the bay and burning away the stars.

TEN

Buenos Aires

Eva had returned from an afternoon meeting with Chainbridge, to find laid out on her bed, a dozen red roses and stunning evening gown. An ornate gold-edged card read "A car will be waiting for you to take you to a performance of *La Traviata*, Ms. Sheridan. Be ready for 7pm". Ivory and gold opera glasses, vermillion gloves and shoes were on her dresser. Despite the invasion of her privacy she knew Foucault had been drawn to her. In the hotel safe behind reception, along with her winnings, she had stored her clutch bag containing her Mauser pistol and ammunition clip. She had assumed her room would be searched thoroughly by Foucault's people.

Eva bathed and she stared at the ceiling, allowed her thoughts to drift. She wondered if she would be invited to Foucault's private stud on the outskirts of the city. Hapsburg hadn't won, but two other horses owned by Foucault had. He had been in an ebullient mood for the rest of the afternoon.

As she sponged herself, Eva steeled herself into character; the spy, the seductress. She dried herself and opened her travel case, where she had placed the day's race card. Opening it out, she wrote the names memorised of those attending the races in Foucault's private box. She underlined the words 'Senator' and 'Bible'.

She selected a black lace corset and stockings, smoothing out the seams as she smoked a cigarette, before slipping into the dress. It was a perfect fit. At the dresser, she applied her make-up, with every stroke of the lipstick, she built a mental layer, burying the person she was. As a stage actress in the Weimar Republic, she had picked up a tip from an old actor; every layer of greasepaint was a brick for the construction of your role. She applied her blush and gave her eyes a smoky, smouldering look.

She sprayed a fine mist of perfume and stepped in and out of it. Then lastly, she fastened her ivory handle stiletto knife along her inside thigh. Her compact contained a swing blade and her lipstick cap contained three cyanide pills. She decided to leave the gun in the safe.

Until later.

She found Chainbridge in a back room behind the hotel bar where a poker game was well under way. He was in a shirt, tie loosened, trilby tilted back and his hawk-like features engrossed in the game. The other players were horse trainers, two of whom she'd photographed earlier. He glanced up and winked at her. She stood at the table, and the men whistled appreciatively and raised their glasses.

"Off to the opera tonight!" she grinned, giving a twirl.

Chainbridge raised an eyebrow.

"Mr. Foucault, I presume."

The men grinned and some tipped knowing winks to one another.

"Eligible bachelor, Eileen, you might be the one for him!" piped up one.

"This is a purely professional meeting!" she feigned a blush. Reaching into her clutch, she handed over the folded race card.

"Now don't go blowing our retainers, Jameson!" she said.

"Oh, I forgot, you dropped this earlier."

Chainbridge handed her a silver brooch, a Celtic fox, contained within it was a fast acting toxin, the fox's flowing tail concealing the needle point.

"Thank you, James. Good night boys!" she waved as she clipped out of the bar to the man waiting to escort her to the opera.

Clever girl, thought Chainbridge, plenty of witnesses here.

***

The Teatro Colón's Romanesque colonnades and dizzying stained glass dome was the perfect backdrop for the assembled dignitaries gathered for the opera. Foucault guided Eva on his arm through the throng, with Menzies following close in tow. Eva's eyes flitted around Foucault's entourage; the pug-faced security man from the marquee was a few paces off them along with a few 'security chaps'. They all spoke with English accents.

The box was plush, darkened and gave a sweeping view of the stage. Champagne sat in the bucket, a Dom Pérignon 1921, Eva noted as she was offered a fan. Foucault, though close to her, didn't make her uncomfortable. They had an unspoken ease between them. He was dressed in formal attire with a white silk bow tie, crisp shirt and not a hair out of place. They sat in a companionable silence as the orchestra began to tune up and the stalls began to fill.

"I'm told the acoustics here are as good as La Scala," his voice, though always pitched low, was clear and distinct.

"I was there before the war," said Eva "Molajoli conducting *'La Gioconda'*. I'm looking forward to it."

"Ah, 1939, I believe, I saw that performance, too. It's amazing we didn't meet."

He smiled, she liked it; it was genuine and started from his eyes.

"So Eileen, you're an aficionado then? Do you play?"

"Piano."

"Well, if you're interested, I have one on my yacht. I'd love to hear you play."

She smiled in return, though cast her eyes downward, an effective lure along with her pitching her voice low.

"I'd love to Charles."

Before the overture began and the lights began to dim, she panned the opera glasses around the auditorium and a flash of blonde hair in one of the boxes opposite made her flick back. There was a granite-faced man in the box with a shaved pate, seemingly ironed into his evening wear and the gloved arm of a woman, the rest of her immersed in shadows. Eva studied the man, a man who would look more comfortable placing wagers at a dog fight than an opera. Unsettled, Eva pretended to immerse herself into the production.

From her vantage point, Hannah Wolfe studied Eva from the shadows. She leaned back and sighed; she was bored. Bausch was poor company, a dour automaton who viewed her with borderline disdain. She watched the opera with mild interest, keeping within the shadows.

Menzies entered the booth.

"We're bringing her to the boat."

ELEVEN

The Manzana de las luces, Buenos Aires

"It's a modified type of Bakelite," said the Jesuit.

Brandt, Chainbridge and Curran stared at the piece of the packing shell that Brandt had brought with him from the dry dock. They were sitting in the outer offices of the Father Provincial in the Jesuit mission at the Plaza de Mayo. The room was more of a cell, with a small window through which the morning sunlight filtered onto a modest cross of ebony. The black-cassocked Jesuit who had taken the fragment of tubing into the mission had returned within fifteen minutes and placed it delicately on the table in the middle of the room. Chainbridge held the fragment up to the light, turning it over again and again. Then he handed it to Brandt.

"And these were tubes you say?"

"Yes, placed end-to-end, the length of each side of the vessel. Twenty-eight in total, each several metres long, increasing in height until they were about twice mine." replied Brandt.

"Why would Foucault be transporting Bakelite?" enquired Curran.

"I'm not a sailor, but the sheets around the hull didn't look right to me, maybe the photographs I took might show something," said Brandt.

"Father Alvarez is quite an enthusiastic photographer. Will the pictures have developed by now?"

Fr. Alvarez bowed slightly with a smile.

"I'll check now. May I offer you gentlemen some coffee?" His voice was soft, musical but also assured. He was as thin as an El Greco study.

"Please."

Chainbridge sat in a chair facing the desk. Curran and Brandt leaned in studying the Bakelite fragment in the lamplight. Curran appeared at home in the silent, dark wood panelled room.

"Once a man of the cloth?" Chainbridge asked.

"In a former life, Chainbridge, the Irish Civil war changed all that, but I still have some useful connections."

Alvarez came back in with a silver tray, with a highly-polished silver coffee pot and delicate china cups. He placed it onto the desk, under his arm was a leather portfolio which he opened out.

"Most were unusable," he glanced over at Brandt, "but luckily, we got two."

Alvarez placed the two photographs on the desk.

"There," pointed Chainbridge. Above the canvas skirt around the hull of the vessel were what appeared to be deep grooves in the vessel's hull, "what are those?"

"I don't know," murmured Curran. "Mr. Brandt, any ideas?"

"They were hoisting the tubes with cranes and trying to position them. The tubes length gave the crane operator some problems. They are behind schedule."

"And Japanese navy too?" said Chainbridge.

Brandt nodded.

"Weapons components for the Japanese? Where is her next port of call?" asked Curran holding a photograph to the light.

"Marseilles," said Brandt.

"The German Navy's deep water U-boat port. What the bloody hell is Foucault up to?" said Chainbridge.

"There's one other thing, the German foremen had access to an industrial plant on the dry dock. I could see big containers with lots of heavy welding and rivets. They were stamped: 'Vorsicht!- U-235' in stencil."

"Uranium," said Alvarez without any hesitation. The three men looked up at him, he slid his arms into the folds of his cassock.

"I've a degree in physics."

"Fissile material," said Chainbridge.

"It's not a U-boat we're looking for, Henry, it's a gun, a bloody big gun. Maybe they're disguising the barrels with the Bakelite," said Brandt. His voice seemed to bounce around the white-washed walls as he spoke. "The Wehrmacht had some designs before the war involving some sort of super-gun. Maybe they've dusted down the files."

Chainbridge looked again at the photographs on the table.

"We need to stop that ship leaving Buenos Aires."

***

Eva hit the chill waters face first, shocking her awake. She was drowning. Her body reflexed into kicking her legs upwards. She gagged in the air, and violently coughed up the saltwater of the bay. Her head felt split in two from the blow she had received to the back of her head. She was losing consciousness again. Fighting the desire to sleep, she pulled off her gloves and discarded them. Her dress was dragging her back into the depths, a leaden weight around her. Treading water unsteadily, she found her stiletto still strapped to her thigh. Releasing the clasp, she retrieved it and commenced cutting her dress away. She kicked it away from her. Dawn was just on the horizon and she could finally get her bearings in the faint light.

"Leave her to the sharks," was the last thing she'd heard from Foucault before being struck. She blacked out again momentarily; she could feel her mouth filling with water. It tasted of oil and ships' waste. In the grips of an increasing panic, she clutched the stiletto, took a deep draught of air and submerged. With quick movements she ran the blade along the corsets laces at the back. She felt the sharp nick of the blade against her skin. Once free of the garment, she surfaced and looked around. Her teeth were chattering. In the distance Foucault's yacht *Serenity* steamed away, heading out into the Atlantic Ocean, her lights ablaze.

Eva looked around her; in the distance, the lights of Buenos Aires twinkled in the dawn light as distant from her now as the stars still overhead in the sky. She had no option, she had to swim. Images started to appear as flash-backs; the standing ovations at the opera, the limousine and the sumptuous champagne supper aboard the luxury yacht with Foucault and his entourage. The last thing she remembered was watching Menzies collapse with her silver brooch wedged in his throat. The toxin within it had acted fast, killing him before he'd hit the carpet. Then she had punched Hannah Wolfe hard in the face, before she had been grabbed and everything had gone white, then the pitch black of the abyss.

As she swam, Eva focussed all her energy into every stroke, every breath toward the distant lights. She forced herself to be calm. Her head throbbed, pumping blood into the bay. If the sharks got her so be it, but if she got out in one piece, she was going to kill Foucault. She couldn't bring herself to think of Brandt, because those thoughts alone would overwhelm her.

Cold-blooded revenge was the spur.

Serenity was now a bright dot on the sea, her rigging catching the morning sunlight.

Eva had to pause, her muscles ached from her exertions and the first worms of doubt began gnawing at her. The shore lights were a good distance away and her vision began to blur. Her thoughts began to drift and before she began to slip under, she wondered what would Brandt have made of her ending up like this?

As she began to sink, inertia taking hold, a bow wave pushed her forward. She felt hands under her arms and being lifted from the water. Her legs gave way on the deck of a small fishing vessel and a heavy, foul-smelling overcoat thrown over her. Eva opened her eyes and saw the ruddy, creased features of an old fisherman staring at her.

"No hospital, no hospital…" she murmured in Spanish.

"OK, my pretty little mermaid, then where to?" He replied in English.

He rose and adjusted the sail trim. Looking out over the bow of the small vessel, he nodded, "Sharks."

"There always are..," she propped herself up and watched the wicked fins gliding through the surface nearby. "I need to get to Buenos Aires."

"No problem. But please try to stay awake."

"Easier said than done," and with that Eva dozed off.

She was back in Foucault's state room aboard *Serenity*, it was accessed by the sweeping onyx and black marble staircase. The room had deep wood panelling and heavy wooden antique desk; a backdrop of black, red and luscious deep green drapes that covered the portholes and doorways, masking any sound. She thought Foucault had consumed enough champagne to incapacitate himself – she was wrong. When she looked up from the schematics lifted from the drawer she had jimmied open, he was standing there with Hannah and Menzies.

"That's hardly the human interest piece we were discussing; I must have words with your editor, whoever that is," he said.

"You should be more careful with your papers – selling weapons to the Germans? Not very patriotic," she replied.

"The question you need to ask yourself, Miss Sheridan is, am I indiscreet or was that left for you to find?" said Foucault.

Eva held his gaze, she thought she saw a flicker of unease.

"Enough to suggest your actions are treason," she said.

"But very profitable," he stood elegant in French cuffs, ornate cuff links and his Rolex. His evening jacket, loosened bow tie and slender slacks gave him an assured dissoluteness. Hannah stood hour-glass in satin; they made a devilish couple.

"Gauleiter Guy Michelet, was he at the races today? – should I know him?" asked Eva.

"His name is immaterial now, Miss Sheridan. You won't be making his acquaintance," said Foucault.

Menzies had smiled, it reminded Eva of a faithful guard dog, hovering in the background waiting for the slightest signal from its owner. He was panting, waiting for the nod.

"We finally meet at face-to-face at last," said Hannah.

"I should have killed you in Tuscany," said Eva.

"Yes, you should have, Molenaar, that is your name? Am I correct?" said Hannah. She was sewn into her evening dress, thought Eva, with a corset underneath, it would be like a piece of armour; but that in itself would restrict her movements.

"Let's make this interesting, shall we?" said Foucault.

He dragged a solid looking high backed art nouveau chair into the middle of the room.

"Get some rope and Herr Bausch," he said to Menzies, "I believe he has certain methods learned at Bad Tölz that may prove useful."

Eva had held up her hands, as she did so, she had released the silver fox brooch from her dress.

"I'm a journalist, not a spy as the lady there suggests - what's here should be public knowledge; an English Lord and a French Gauleiter conspiring against the Allies with The Waffen S.S," she said.

She thumbed the fox's tail open.

"This ship has an infirmary, why not take her there?" said Hannah, "strap her down and let me at her."

"Always a rich man's plaything – how does that feel?" said Eva.

Hannah glared.

"At least you have dropped the pretence. I have a few methods of my own – I'll soften her up for Viktor," she had said.

Then she had stormed toward Eva as Menzies left the room.

Foucault had sat down in the chair he just pulled to the centre of the room to watch the women fight.

The liquid burning her insides woke Eva. It was a strong brandy and she felt the ceramic spout placed over her lips.

"Drink."

The old fisherman looked at her; a beautiful young woman, naked, except for a knife sheath strapped to her thigh. In the oversized coat, she appeared small and vulnerable. He had spied her swimming a few hundred yards out when by sheer luck, her pale arms had caught the sunrise. Trimming the sails, he had caught her just in time; her final strokes had been nothing more than flailing around. She had an open wound to her head, onto which he had poured the brandy. She had a knife wound in the small of her back, but a superficial one.

"I had a knife."

"It's gone." For some reason, the loss of the stiletto brought stinging tears to her eyes.

"Thank you." The alcohol warmed her up, yet, she felt drained and ill. "Can you get me to a hotel without me being seen?"

"My brother-in-law owns a bakery. We can put you in the back of the delivery van. Which hotel?"

"The Cosmopolitan."

The old man whistled.

"Must've been one hell of a party."

"It was."

TWELVE
Serenity

Foucault dined on a fine breakfast in the company of Hannah Wolfe in *Serenity*'s stately dining room. She had spent the remainder of the night with Foucault. Hannah's upper lip had been split by Eva before Bausch had swung the heavy crystal ashtray across the back of Eva's head. Foucault had tenderly dabbed Hannah's lip with a silk handkerchief before kissing her; he seemed to like the taste of blood. He had a tattoo under his left armpit – blood group, Nazi racial profile number and an intricately detailed lion, draped in the Union Jack.

"How are you feeling this morning, my dear?" He gave off the manner of a distant, mildly concerned doctor. Hannah remembered that.

"She shouldn't have been killed like that. I'd have preferred her alive," her lip felt swollen, and her two front teeth had loosened; it made her mood foul.

"She was nothing more than an inconvenience, Hannah, if we have to deal with it, we'll tell the authorities she fell overboard during a party. I'm well known for my licentious soirees!" He leered at her over his poached eggs and steamed asparagus.

Hannah was one of those girls that whichever way she moved, no amount of clothing could conceal her smooth, luscious flesh. As for her lovemaking, it was perfunctory, but not without its possibilities. He had visualised Eva and Hannah pleasuring each other as Hannah had straddled him; *t'was a pity Eva was dead*, he thought.

The ornate telephone rang. Foucault reached for the receiver and listened for a few moments.

"Thank you," he looked at Hannah, "*The Aurora* finally put to sea a few moments ago, the consignment is secure."

He dialled up the radio room.

"Have Miss Sheridan's effects brought to my private quarters. Also, send a team to deal with her colleague, Mr. Williams. Make the necessary arrangements."

He looked at Hannah.

"If she was Allied intelligence, then Williams – or whatever his name is – was a handler. Best snip off any loose threads."

Hannah took a cigarette from an ornate cigarette case on the table.

"Is it possible to capture him instead?"

"Why? It's just another spy; the graveyards are full of them."

***

Eva was back in Berlin again; it was May 1933. Pyres of books blazed in the night. She was running from her pursuers, two drunken SA troopers, through the corridors of Humboldt University. As she ran, Eva could see all the faces of everyone she had ever known; her parents, grandparents, cousins and friends. As she passed them they ignited and turned to ash. The troopers chasing her finally cornered her. One of them had the face of Foucault.

She snapped awake in a sweat. There were voices that sounded above her, like a drone. After a moment, she recognised the words.

"She has a serious concussion. Without an X-ray, I can't rule out a fracture." The woman's voice was strong, assured and when Eva's vision cleared, a nun was looking down on her.

Eva propped herself up. She looked around; she was in a small room, like a monk's cell. Around her cot stood Chainbridge, the severe looking nun, a tall thin man in tweeds and behind him, a Jesuit priest. A troika of rites.

"This girl must rest for a few days," said the nun. Her lips didn't seem to move. Her complexion had the ruddy softness of an old maid.

"Thank you, Sister. Is she fit to fly?" Chainbridge asked.

"No. She is not fit to fly." Said the nun.

"I feel fine. I'm ok." Eva sipped the water offered by Chainbridge; the water was cool, her tongue felt swollen.

"I'm afraid, Sister Oliver, she needs to fly out tonight."

With the whisk of starch, the nun left the room.

"We cleared out of the hotel after you were reported missing. How do you feel?" asked Chainbridge.

"Good, all things considered," her vision was blurred and her skull ached down to the base of the neck.

"This is Curran and this is Fr. Alvarez, Eva, may I ask what happened?"

"I was attacked soon after I boarded."

Curran regarded her with borderline contempt.

"Did you manage to hear anything? Anything useful?" It carried in his voice.

Eva paused. She remembered one thing before Bausch took the swing.

"The American warship in the bay, *The U.S.S. Iowa*. She's due in Egypt in late October. President Roosevelt will be on board."

"Anything else?" Chainbridge had never seen Eva in such a wretched condition. He watched her as she struggled to think. Curran exhaled impatiently, like an Inquisitor Generalis, he wanted rid of her. Alvarez studied her, his demeanour that of a man who didn't like women either.

"Marseilles. Both vessels the *Serenity* and *The Aurora* are outward bound to Marseilles. Due to arrive in and around the same day. They are shipping a weapon. A big one, requires both ships. Foucault has received a substantial amount of gold-bullion for the shipment."

"What has he done with the bullion?" asked Curran.

"I don't know," replied Eva.

"Marseilles, it is then gentlemen. London's four hours ahead, we'd better get word to the Admiralty and GHQ India; Egypt and Persia's on their watch," said Chainbridge.

"The Americans?" asked Curran,

"We don't know the nature of the threat, we can guess. Best let Director Hoover know anyway," said Chainbridge.

"He dropped the ball with Pearl Harbour, I'll get word to the President's people through another channel," said Curran.

Eva looked at Chainbridge.

"Henry, where's Brandt?"

THIRTEEN

The South Atlantic, Aurora

Brandt and Carrington sat together in the *Aurora*'s mess. Around them, the ship's crew sat reading or playing cards. For the past two days, the *Aurora* seemed to be vibrating from bow to stern, fighting the sea. Without warning the ship rolled wildly, spilling plates of food and cups off tables. The more experienced tars lifted their arms, still keeping their cards concealed as pewter plates and mugs clattered onto the floor.

Brandt was taking a break from the graveyard shift. His cabin-mate, the senior engineer, a bearded Afrikaan by the name of Jongbloed, seemed more interested in brewing his own moonshine. Jongbloed had smuggled aboard several crates of white grapes, stuffed into every spare crevice of the cabin along with his makeshift still. The sour-sweet smell was impossible to get rid of from Brandt's nostrils.

"I bru Witblits. Drink," was all he said when Brandt had been assigned to engineering.

Judging by the liquid's taste, it was going to be a short journey for the South African.

Brandt prayed that the brawny, middle-aged Afrikaan engineer wouldn't drop dead on the voyage. The ship pitched starboard and several of the crew vomited violently onto the mess floor.

"I love a leisurely cruise. Pulled the graveyard shift, I see, Hauk," said Carrington. He gripped the table's edge with one huge hand whilst trying to drink from a chipped mug.

Carrington had handed the Warrant Officer a wad of US dollars, telling a story of a cuckolded husband who had put a contract out on him. The Warrant Officer, a granite-faced Englishman named Sheppard, had smiled in a knowing manner,

"Not English, Aussie?" asked Sheppard.

"Close – New Zealand." Said Carrington.

"We've a load of colonials aboard." Said Sheppard. He slipped the money into the folds of his jacket and signed Carrington on.

Pryce had spoken to Sheppard and agreed Brandt would sign on as an unlicensed rating.

"Might keep the engineer on his toes." Grinned Sheppard

Brandt's first duties had been to swab out the latrines.

"Have you seen or heard anything?" asked Brandt.

Carrington glanced around.

"Nothing. Though most of the holds and lower decks are protected by armed 'contractors' – Japanese contractors. They're berthed in the lower decks, near the secured holds."

Pryce, wheeled past with the assurance of an ice skater, his feet seemingly welded to the deck plates.

"We're battening down the hatches, lads," he said.

The ship lurched starboard again. It seemed to fall for a very long time before righting herself.

"Storm's getting' worse," said Carrington.

"Best report to the engine room," murmured Brandt as he swilled the dregs of his coffee. He could taste the ship's aged metal pipes in the brew.

In the engine room, Jongbloed was staring at the diesel engines in a manner that suggested he had instantly sobered up. The heat was sapping; Brandt's overalls were drenched in sweat.

"Too much drag," intoned the South African. If Jongbloed was nervous, there was a very good reason to be.

"Drag?"

Jongbloed barked a series of orders to Brandt; he assumed Brandt was a complete idiot handling his beloved engines.

On several occasions, they were knocked off their feet by the force of the storm, which was met with guttural Afrikaan oaths. Sea water seeped in around their boots from the water-tight doors, Brandt looked overhead with his heart in his mouth. The fear of drowning like some rat in a cage overwhelmed him. His thoughts turned to Eva, and for a moment, he thought he'd never see her again. He was soon slapped back to reality.

"We have work to do, Hauk! Get back to your duties you lazy fuggin' hond!"

"Why are we pushing the vessel so hard?" roared Brandt over the noise. His ears were waddled with cotton wool.

"The captain wants to keep up with Lord-high-and-mighty, fuggin' Foucault's yacht. This blasted rust-bucket is no match for her," roared Jongbloed.

"Yacht?" shouted Brandt.

"The fuggin' *Serenity*," roared Jongbloed.

Serenity, thought Brandt. Carrington and Pryce were aboard to track her.

The Aurora had smashed through the storm, not without jarring moments when the diesels ground metal on metal and screamed in protest. Jongbloed's nerve held and Brandt's attention had kept everything moving. The South African had nursed the ship through with curses, pleas, blows from a huge wrench along with prayers, grease and sheer skill. Several hours later, Brandt climbed into his bunk, drained and aching.

Now he had to think of way to sabotage the engines.

Jongbloed carried a lethal fisherman's reefer knife at all times. Brandt carried Carrington's army knife. If it came to a fight, the South African would probably win. His thoughts were broken by Jongbloed's grizzly features appearing beside his bunk.

"We're wanted topside."

"Christ! Now?"

"Yes, now, Hauk. Move your arse."

Serenity slowed her engines to a stop. Hannah could feel the ship's momentum gradually slowing down. The suite's lavish wooden flooring had the *sonnenrad* symbol inlaid into it with ebony. It was the identical design as in Himmler's Wewelsburg Castle; a wheel with twelve broken spokes radiating from the centre.

"The black sun; the axis mundi of Nazi ideology," Himmler had told her when she had been promoted to the rank of SS. Scharführer. "We are the last standing bulwark against the Jewish threat of Bolshevism, the defenders of the light."

Like Himmler's chambers, Foucualt's suite had twelve pillars encircling the plush leather settees, coffee tables and sumptuous library. Overhead, hung an immense crystal chandelier. Pride of place on the suite's wall was a portrait of Hitler, posing in medieval armour. Hannah had no interest in books, though she idly thumbed the pages of a Hollywood periodical.

Foucault was at his antique desk, running through his 'morning constitutional'. Every morning for the past week, he had begun is day – even in the teeth of the storm that they had battered their way through. This ritual began every morning after breakfast with eye drops of liquid cocaine and various injections from a supply of gold-foiled vitamins recommended by Hitler's personal physician: Theodor Morell. Foucault was so enamoured with the Führer, he learned everything he could about him and imitated his habits.

"Can I offer you a spot of invigoration, my dear?" he asked. He wrapped his tourniquet and phials back into his desk.

"No."

"Very well, my dear, I feel just capital now, now let's have a look at that little Hellion's effects, shall we?"

He produced from a drawer Eva's passport, lipstick, compact and shoes. Foucault held up the shoes in admiration, they were of excellent craftsmanship. He then fiddled with her lipstick, releasing a catch, several pea-sized pills fell out and scattered across the desk.

"Cyanide," said Hannah, without looking up.

"The little minx," he murmured. No question about it, Miss Eileen Sheridan was an allied spy.

Foucault placed everything back into the drawer and locked it. He asked Hannah for her heavy leather-bound spy list. He eyed her ample curves as she rose lithely from the settee and handed the folder to him in a fluid movement. She was a fine little filly, he thought. He worked his way through the lists of photographs, finding Eva Molenaar.

He removed the photograph.

"May I keep this, my dear?"

"Yes."

There was a knock at the door and a uniformed seaman saluted.

"*Aurora* is alongside, sir."

"About time too; must have a word with their captain; two days behind since leaving port is unacceptable; maybe they should jettison some of the cargo. Excellent, Excellent. Fancy a spot of sport, my dear? Grab a heavy coat."

***

Brandt blinked in the weak sunlight having been below decks for almost a week. The clouds boiled overhead and a squall burst flashed on the far horizon. The seas had calmed, though the freighter still rode them uneasily. Starboard side, *Serenity* appeared close by. Brandt could see a flurry of activity aboard her. *The Aurora* sat low in the water, her decks lower than some of the yachts upper decks. Jongbloed stood alongside Brandt, red-eyed and taking fortifying nips from his bottle. *The Aurora*'s Captain, a taciturn man named Eklund, his senior officers and engineers stood in a knot beside them.

"I don't like this, Hauk. Don't like it at all," said Jongbloed, he handed Brandt a swig.

"I agree." Brandt's well-honed instincts put him on edge.

As he scratched his full, oil-stained beard, his eyes flicked around and sipped the lethal brew. One of *The Aurora*'s forward hatches opened, from it emerged the crewmen in single file. Twenty men led by Sheppard and Pryce stood on the deck, some chatting, smoking and pointing over at the yacht. Others stretched their legs and began to stroll along the deck, one of them was Carrington, a full head and shoulders above the rest of the men.

Brandt glanced back at the yacht. It had pulled in alongside and he could make out the faces of five people standing at the rails. They were all brandishing rifles. A scream came from the deck below Brandt and Jongbloed. A group of ten Japanese men bolted from the superstructure, stripped to the waist and brandishing samurai swords. They set upon the surprised sailors. Shouts and screams rose as the stunned sailors were massacred. Severed limbs and heads fell into the sea as the blades flashed and glinted.

From *Serenity*'s deck, Hannah took careful aim and picked off two stragglers who broke away from the attacking Japanese. Bausch and Foucault were shooting into the melee with deliberate satisfaction. Beside them, stood two liveried stewards, stationed either side of a mobile, well stocked, walnut gun rack. Two sailors dived headfirst into the sea. Hannah readjusted the sights on her rifle; a Walther Gewehr 41, took careful aim and killed the men when they surfaced.

Foucault's aim was equal to the task and he yelled with glee after several successful kills. Bausch grunted after each shot, cursing after a missing a tall man loping along the deck. He waited for a moment. The man's head popped up for a beat, long enough for Bausch to squeeze the trigger.

Carrington fell, the top of his head blown off. Brandt clenched his teeth in anger. Below him, the decks were awash with blood as the last of the sailors were cruelly dispatched. Two Spaniards were forced to their knees and one of the Japanese, barking orders, clearly in charge, beheaded them in two swift strokes with his sword. He saluted the marksmen on the other vessel.

Sheppard's and Pryce' bodies were the last ones heaved over the side along with the knots of severed limbs that littered the deck.

Nagasawa bounded up the stairwell, his arms and upper body streaked with blood. Brandt recognised a blood-frenzy and gripped the knife he had hidden up the sleeve of his boiler suit.

Jongbloed slipped the long, thin reefer knife out from his overalls.

"I'm going to fix that little shit," he murmured.

Nagasawa began shouting at the Captain, pointing his long sword toward Brandt and Jongbloed repeatedly and pointing toward the deck with it. Brandt sensed the Afrikaan was going to charge.

Taking a slow breath, Brandt strode forward and started barking at Eklund.

"Who the hell is this man? Why did he massacre the crew?"

"Orders from *Serenity*. No witnesses." Eklund buried his creased features deep into the folds of his thick, greatcoat. Brandt had to force him to make eye contact, gripping the lapels.

"Let me spell this out to you, Captain Eklund, you drove this bloody ship too hard in the storm. The number one diesel has only forty per cent capacity and the number two diesel has a serious fracture along the driveshaft. Killing me and senior engineer Jongbloed will seriously affect the voyage, I doubt if any of those Japs could operate them. Killing Sheppard and Pryce was foolish too, who is going to crew the bloody ship?"

Nagasawa's eyes narrowed toward Brandt as he adjusted his stance to attack, blade raised. Brandt stepped forward, the man was shorter than Brandt, he could smell sweat, garlic, bad breath and blood coming off the Japanese in waves.

"Tell this prick to stand down!" Brandt spat. He moved closer. He switched hands and the knife was poised to strike down on the veins bulging out of the man's neck. Their eyes locked; Brandt's clear, focussed, the Japanese, bloodshot and glassy.

"Now, Eklund!" Brandt shouted.

Eklund started talking in hurried Japanese. The man, deprived of fresh kills began ranting and waving his sword around. Brandt wished he had a gun. After much placating, the Japanese man stepped away; not without giving Brandt a threatening glance. Brandt gave him a thin murderous smile. Later.

"Notify *Serenity* that the engine room has been spared…for now. This 'prick' as you call him is a Lieutenant and his men are Imperial Japanese Navy, they are well equipped to handle this freighter."

"You're a prince, bet one of them wouldn't bother to clean the shithouse like I do," muttered Brandt.

He strode back and gripping Jongbloed's arm began hustling him toward the stairwell that led to the engineering section.

"We're going to die," said Jongbloed.

"Not today, Jongbloed, not today," said Brandt.

Brandt recalled the man who murdered Carrington, a shaven headed prime Aryan specimen. The blonde woman too. Who the hell were they? Their attention was drawn by the signalling coming from the yacht. The freighter's klaxons began wailing. The leader of the Japanese joined his men and began pointing furiously and barking orders. They ran to positions along the freighter's sides.

Jongbloed groaned.

"It just gets better."

Two U-Boats surfaced off the freighter's bow. Their grey, lethal lines cut through the swells as they drew alongside. The U-boats hatches opened and the crews from the submarine's conning towers began flashing semaphore code to the ships.

"What are they saying?" asked Jongbloed.

"Ready to escort," translated Brandt. "They're German."

FOURTEEN
Berlin

Martin Bormann, the squat head of the Parteiknzlei wrote one word on the blotting paper: STALINGRAD. He underlined the word and smiled; surrender and humiliation for Hitler. Goering, Goebbels, Speer and even the mighty Himmler had all been blamed by the Führer. Unlike the letters on the blotting paper these men had shrunk.

He took the paper from the crocodile skin desk blotter and threw it in the bin. He wrote a new word on another piece of blotting paper: Reichsbank. Below it, the word Reichsmark then repeated the letters RM across the width of the page – RM RM RM RM RM RM RM RM RM RM RM RM RM RM RM RM RM RM RM RM RM RM RM RM.

Again the ink was absorbed by the blotting paper and as the letters grew, so would his fortune.

Bormann laughed. He stood up and faced the full length mirror opposite his desk.

The white shirt caught his Adams apple and he adjusted his pencil tie. Because of his bulk, Bormann hated wearing military uniform. He buttoned his brown tweed jacket and checked that the shoulder holster didn't bulge.

In the corner of the room sat SS-Obergruppenführer, Kurt Dietrich Hoeberichts, overall commander of Urus Martan. He was clad in black and leather, pristine and funereal. His hat, sitting beside the coffee set and ashtray, was black Russian sable with the death's head insignia of his regiment. His eyes were heterochromatic, his complexion like Nosferatu.

"I will miss the fashion show in Paris, Reichsleiter Borman," said Hoeberichts.

"The Führer wants civilisation throughout his empire," said Bormann. "You are adjusting to Berlin?"

"I have been here two days."

"And you are already bored?"

Neither man laughed.

Bormann turned away from the full length mirror.

"The Führer wants to meet you in Rastenburg. You will see him alone," said Bormann.

"Not Berlin?" said Hoeberichts. He thought of the lengthy journey by armoured train to get here.

"No, not Berlin."

"I am honoured."

Bormann returned to his desk. He looked down at the used blotting paper in the bin at the side of his desk. Bormann smiled at Hoeberichts. He imagined the commander of Urus Martan searching his bin and reading the blotting paper. It did not matter. The words alone meant nothing.

"The U-235 will be prepared by the Uranprojeckt team at a secure location outside Marseilles, Obergruppenführer. Your contact will be Guy Michelet. He has a passion for falconry.'

"I know nothing of falconry," said Hoeberichts.

"He will not expect you to talk about falconry," said Bormann.

"The targeting system will be explained?"

"In a few days, your command will have the details then."

"I could ask Michelet to explain."

"You could but I wouldn't. Michelet is not a gifted communicator."

"Perhaps I should have stayed in Paris."

Bormann remembered the blotting paper in his waste paper bin and the letters RM stretched across the page. The cost had been staggering; *it would have been cheaper to build the Eagle's nest on the moon*, thought Bormann. For their part, the Abwehr were building a painfully slow intelligence brief to the whereabouts of the location for the next allied conference. With Stalin finally enjoying the taste of victory, Churchill and Roosevelt would be dancing to his tune. The location of the conference would be on his terms.

"Well, two of them would be dancing," he muttered.

"I believe *'Thor's Hammer'* will be capable of firing a uranium projectile into another country," said the Obergruppenführer proudly. "We wiped a Red division out from the other side of Russia with an improved Krupps railway gun. *'Thor's Hammer'* is four times the size; anything is possible, these days."

He stood a full head and shoulders above Bormann, who noted the bejewelled shashka knife secured in an ornate sheath.

"You've been too long out in the Caucuses, Obergruppenführer."

"Too Long. LeLong."

"Long?"

"Lucien LeLong. I met him once before the war in Paris."

"Who is he?" Bormann asked idly.

"He is haute couture, Reichsleiter. He is Paris."

The Obergruppenführer's sheep-dog eyes stared out into the middle distance.

"Such pretty girls."

"I have a plane waiting. Your staff car will be here in a few minutes."

"I have to prepare for my meeting."

"We will both be well prepared."

"Of course."

Once the Führer had given the go-ahead, Bormann planned to take a very pretty girl, an actress named Marianne who Goebbels had cast in his up-coming cinema feature 'Münchhausen', for a romantic weekend in Paris.

That was Goebbels' solution to every set-back; make a bloody movie.

Obergruppenführer Kurt Dietrich Hoeberichts took the blotting paper from the Reichsleiter's waste bin and eased himself back into the large leather chair. He produced from his tunic a silver hip flask. Unscrewing the cap, he poured a shot of vodka into it. He snorted the shot loudly, then dabbed his upper lip delicately.

"Too long in the Caucuses," he said holding the blotting paper up.

FIFTEEN
London

The flying boat had landed in London, mooring at the quayside of Chelsea docks. A car was waiting to take them to Int.7. Inside the grey neo-classical building on the grounds of the University of London, Bracken's Spartan office had a modern, cold feel. Chainbridge looked around the room; Bracken the propagandist, had reams of posters and flyers for approval neatly stacked against the wall. Newspaper articles and texts of forthcoming broadcasts were edited with neat strokes of a fountain pen on a nearby trestle table. Int.7 was a sub-office for the wily Minister without portfolio and by its very anonymity, a very powerful one.

The large conference table was cleared. Chainbridge, Eva and Curran examined Brandt's photographs and segment of Bakelite with Bracken. Curran produced from his pocket a small blue book. The cover had a lion holding a sabre, with a crown hovering above its back.

It was titled: 'Pocket guide to Iran'.

"I received this copy from a contact in the American navy," he said.

"The next conference must be close to being decided," said Chainbridge, as he thumbed through the pocket booklet.

The Allied forces would be cheek to jowl with their Soviet counterparts if it was Tehran. "The Abwehr finding this out will be inevitable," he said.

"We've gone through the names you gave Chainbridge, Miss Molenaar," said Bracken. "Guy Michelet, is of special interest."

"He lost heavily on the races," replied Eva.

"A mere bagatelle for him, Miss Molenaar," said Bracken

He studied the tall, beautiful woman before him. Her personal file pointed to an illustrious academic career had war not broken out. Her presence, though, made the dour Curran distinctly uncomfortable.

"He's involved in high finance, dealing in war bonds, shares and stowing away Vichy bullion on an international level. He is rumoured to have a huge storage facility in Senegal where plunder from the East has been shipped. His chateau outside Marseilles recently underwent a refurbishment, notably his enormous concrete wine cellars. SOE lost two operatives who went to investigate," said Curran.

"He'll be prepared." Said Chainbridge.

"Miss Molenaar, we need you liaise with him," said Bracken.

"It'd be my pleasure," replied Eva.

"I'll talk to the PM this morning, see if we get the two ships stopped and searched. De Witte has confirmed they are both sailing under the Spanish flag, making them neutral vessels." Said Bracken.

At the mention of Peter de Witte's name, Eva's heart gave an unexpected leap. The last time she saw him he had been rescued from Berlin and ill with pneumonia, hiding in a safe house in Zurich. They had once been lovers, now that seemed a lifetime ago.

"Here's the address of a private hospital I keep on retainer. Take a few days' rest and allow the medical team to check you out."

"I feel fine, Mr. Bracken."

"Very well, report to Commando training, Achnacarry, Scotland. You have one week to prepare while we contact the French Resistance. Good luck."

Marseilles, thought Eva, she was sure Brandt would be there.

***

Brandt and Jongbloed had turned the engine room into a veritable fortress. Wrenches, knives, screwdrivers, hammers and anything that might maim an intruder were stashed amid rags, toolboxes or taped into hidden crevices. Brandt had Carrington's knife secured at the small of his back, but wished he had a revolver. Hand-to-hand fighting was a brutal, intimate business and he wondered if the South African was up to it. They were confined to their quarters and the engine room with Eklund ensuring modest quantities of food was sent to them.

"Blasted nips can't make coffee!" hissed the burly engineer as he poured his moonshine into the mug. He hadn't dealt well with the slaughter of the crew and had woken several times in the night, shaking and crying. He thought the gurgling through the pipes was the sound of spilling blood. Brandt had sat up with him, holding his hand, saying nothing. He'd seen men fall apart like this before, once the battle was over and the flashbacks began.

"Is there a way off this ship, Jongbloed? One where we won't be spotted?"

The bleary-eyed engineer sighed.

"No, apart from jumping overboard. Steal a lifeboat and they'd kill you by the time you set the oars up. Besides, we have to refuel in Marseilles and will be moored for about a week, depending on how the engine repairs go. It might be easier to leave then."

"They are going to kill us the moment they sight land. We need an escape plan."

Brandt felt trapped. He had no idea where the Japanese were billeted in the ship and he didn't like the fact he was cornered. The Japanese Lieutenant wouldn't let Brandt facing him down go unpunished, and no doubt an example would be made of him.

His thoughts were broken when the bridge order telegraph shrieked its alarm and the arms on the brass mechanism in the middle of the room cranked and ground over the engine's din to the command 'Dead Stop.'

"Now what?" he muttered.

Captain Eklund and his senior officers viewed the British destroyer as she glided alongside with dread. She was a British L-Class vessel, sleek, neat and lethal. All of her six 120mm guns were trained on *The Aurora* and a boarding party was already making its way toward them. Eklund scanned the horizon for Foucault's yacht; it had made good time and was out of sight. The U-boats had dived the moment the destroyer had appeared and were lurking below *The Aurora*'s keel. All it would take is Ekland to send a single command. He was keen to avoid it.

"Extend every courtesy."

His second-in-command nodded and left the bridge to arrange a welcoming party.

Eklund hoped that Foucault's plan would work. As the armed marines pulled alongside, the Japanese appeared on deck, dressed in overalls; *so much could go wrong in so little time*, Eklund thought. And they were at least three days away from the French coast.

***

Chainbridge re-read the communique; the freighter had been searched and nothing on board had matched Bakelite tubes. The manifest had been checked along with all the paperwork and everything had been in order. The only thing that appeared untoward was the small number of crew, all Korean according to the log. HMS Fortitude had now departed the area.

"Bloody hell."

Curran, Bracken and de Witte sat around a table in Bracken's darkened office. Peter de Witte had joined them at Bracken's request. De Witte, seemed slightly diminished in himself; his handsome features slightly drawn and at times, he struggled for breath. The well-cut slate grey suit hung slightly loose about him.

"We can't be sure Brandt saw these tubes being loaded onto the ship," said Curran.

"And to transport fissile materials would require special heavy containers, again nothing was there to indicate that," agreed Bracken. It was close to midnight and all the buildings had the blackout imposed. The room's windows had heavy drapes drawn and the ghostly wail of air raid sirens drifted in.

"I checked Foucault's yacht's manifest. It wasn't easy, but I have a friend in Lloyds," said de Witte. "*Serenity* is transporting horses and equine pharmaceuticals on board. She's refuelling at Marseilles, before sailing on into occupied Crimea. Do we have the option of having her searched before she reaches there?"

"The Royal Navy is operationally stretched and by now, both vessels will be in Vichy waters."

"We had better send the team into Marseilles and hope Brandt makes it," said Chainbridge.

"Get word to them via your contacts in the Red Orchestra in Zurich, Peter," said Chainbridge. "Marseilles it is then, gentlemen. How's everyone's French?'

***

This is it, thought Brandt, *This is how it ends*. He closed his eyes and inhaled the crisp Atlantic breezes that swept across the deck, savouring the clear air. Along the ship's sides, ropes, chains and pulleys were uncovered from camouflaged tarpaulins. The U-boat crews climbed up the sides, enjoying the air and freedom of

121

the bigger ship's decks. Groups of four men; submariners and Japanese were ordered to stations at equal distances along the deck. Brandt and Jongbloed were with two of the U-boat crewmen, both smoking and telling Brandt they were from the towns of Bremen and Düsseldorf. At a shouted command the group took hold of the ropes and began to haul. Within an hour, the Bakelite tubes that Brandt had seen in the dry dock had been brought up from under *The Aurora*'s keel, where they had been since the ship had departed Buenos Aires. The tubes lay on the decks, glistening like the frigid tentacles of some strange aquatic beast. Nagasawa, checked each of the tubes for fissures or breaks. He was jumpy, methodical and abrupt with his orders. A cold-hearted leader who would be universally hated by his men, thought Brandt.

"At least I wasn't wrong about the ship dragging. We were lucky the engines hadn't seized or hopped off their mountings," said Jongbloed. "What the bloody hell are they?"

"I think they are parts of a very big gun," replied Brandt.

"For whom?"

"Probably the Third Reich."

The Afrikaaner whistled. "What are they going to shoot? The moon?"

The last of the submerged components were hauled aboard. The huge rectangular blocks of Bakelite; the lead-lined containers with the stamped letters U-235, thought Brandt. The Bakelite tubes and containers were lashed together and moved into the centre of the freighter's deck. Once secured everything was wrapped in heavy tarpaulins. Brandt took a light from the submariner from Bremen.

"I've been stuck in the engine room since Buenos Aires, how far are we away from France?"

The thin, bearded submariner exhaled and scratched his dirty, matted beard as he stared out at the sea.

"Good weather for the next few days, Hauk, I'd say two day's tops. We'll be escorting you into the harbour."

Brandt gave him three more cigarettes from his top pocket as a thank you. With a jaunty salute, the Bremen submariner climbed over the side and lowered himself by rope, timing his jump perfectly into the pitching dinghy. The U-boat crews re-joined their vessels and the small flotilla began their final stage of the journey. Brandt played the rope in; one thing about being a mountaineer, he understood ropes and how to use them. Glancing around to ensure he wasn't seen, he took the rope and stored it near the aft section of the ship. There was enough on it for him to jump ship and lower himself onto either a dock or at the worst, into the sea.

Now he just had to settle the score with Nagasawa.

Jongbloed invited the guards into the engineering section for a drink in guttural pidgin Japanese. He waved his bottle of Witblitz at the doorway of the engine room, holding up three mugs. Once inside, Brandt killed them both with Carrington's knife and a heavy wrench.

He took their small Nambu pistols and threw one to Jongbloed.

"Hide the bodies."

Jongbloed froze in disbelief.

"Now. Seal the door, I'll knock four times, at two second intervals."

With that, Brandt, taking a crudely drawn map Jongbloed had made for him, crept toward the Japanese bunks.

Brandt found Nagasawa berating a subordinate in one of the forward holds, lit by a single naked bulb. The Lieutenant was smacking the man around the head, yelling and delivering kicks to the cowering man. Before the startled minion could open his mouth, Brandt shot him in the chest. Nagasawa turned long enough for them to make eye-contact, and then Brandt fired. The Japanese fell, with a bullet hole in his cheek. Brandt stood over him and put two shots into Nagasawa's forehead at point-blank range. Wiping the gun on his shirt, he placed it in the hand of the groaning, injured subordinate who was lying prone on the floor. He found Nagasawa's service pistol and shot the injured man a second time in the chest, straight into the heart.

He placed the gun in Nagasawa's hand.

Brandt made his way back to engineering above decks as the shouting began.

Jongbloed opened the door after the coded knock.

"We're getting off," said Brandt. "Follow me."

"I can't Hauk, I just can't, the ship needs me."

"Okay, Jongbloed."

Brandt put all his weight behind the punch he delivered to the South African's jaw. Jongbloed crumpled onto the engine room's floor, unconscious. Brandt dragged him into the middle of the room. Removing the Afrikaaner's belt, Brandt tied the inert man's arms behind his back. Taking the red kerchief, he wore around his neck since the start of the voyage, Brandt stuffed it into the unconscious man's mouth.

"Good luck, my friend."

He rolled the big man onto his chest, and gently moved the head to its side. He fished around in the overalls and found the second Nambu. He stuffed it into his belt. He removed Jongbloed's wrist watch. Brandt calculated he would be outdoors for the next twelve hours, exposed and hanging from the side of the ship. He went to his bunk and grabbed both his greatcoat and one of Jongbloed's heavy woollen jumpers.

Glancing up and down the corridor, he climbed quickly and silently up to the decks aft of the freighter.

SIXTEEN

South coast of England

Eva arrived at RAF 687 Selsey, where she was met by Chainbridge. They were driven to a camouflaged hangar where a mottled German Messerschmitt He111H bomber was being readied.

Curran was standing over the flight plan with the two crewmen. He looked up.

"This aircraft got lost over England a few months ago and had to land because it ran out of fuel, she's perfectly intact, and, we updated all her livery. Have you familiarised yourselves with the extraction plan?"

Both nodded.

"The flight crew are Polish; they have volunteered from 301 squadron, both speak fluent German and the aircraft this time, will be carrying extra fuel. You will be met by French resistance; your contact's name is George Sand."

He paused looking at Chainbridge.

"Are you up for this, Henry?"

"Wouldn't miss it for the world, Curran."

"Miss Molenaar?" he rolled the vowels as if they were citric.

Eva nodded.

"Good hunting then, and try to bring Foucault in, unharmed. He is well connected here. We can have a plane into France within three hours, but until it lands, you're on your own."

Under the watchful gaze of the anti-aircraft gunner crews, the He111H accelerated down the runway, banking steeply into the early evening clouds. It flew low across the English Channel to the northern coast of France. Once over Normandy, Eva and Chainbridge glanced at each other. Below them was the Third Reich.

Eva closed her eyes and composed her breathing. Her week in Scotland at Achnacarry had been draining and intense, the only woman amid a group of soldiers, Eva excelled at pistol shooting, and explosives, but her polyglot abilities earned the most grudging respect from her trainers. Hand-to-hand combat had left her bruised from head to toe, Eva insisting the team didn't pull their punches and they duly obliged.

She still felt hung over from the marathon drinking session the night before her departure, where she got up and walked away from the table, leaving the hard men face down amid the whiskey bottles.

"Good luck, Miss." Her staff sergeant, Ramsay had saluted, "just remember, Miss, that Hitler's directive 'Commando order 1942', means if you are captured with SOE paraphernalia, you will be automatically shot."

"I'm Polish, Staff sergeant, Ramsay, it's an automatic death sentence." She replied.

He held her hand a fraction too long, and she allowed him. He was tall, rugged and broad. He was as rough-hewn as the mountains she had passed through and blessed with a gentle burr when he spoke. He had roared obscenities at her as he fired live ammunition above her head as she traversed a rope bridge and then whispered sincere apologies from the corner of his mouth as she scraped the viscous mud from her uniform.

"Come back safe, Miss. We could use a good translator up here." He said.

He finally released his grasp.

"Thank you. Maybe someday." She replied.

She inwardly felt a twist of guilt about Brandt.

"Remember the rip-cord, Miss, you will be free-falling in the dark and you will be disorientated."

"I know, count to twenty and kiss my *arse* goodbye. Are you always this attentive to your recruits, Staff Sergeant Ramsay?" Eva asked.

The big man blushed, adding to his allure.

"They're usually a grubby, ugly bunch, Miss." He replied.

"I'll remember the rip-chord, sir."

"Also, your shovel makes a good weapon, Miss. If all else fails; use it like an axe as you were shown."

With a gallant bow, he kissed her hand and saluted,

"Good hunting, miss."

Ramsay watched her climb into the removal van. It was liveried as a local baker; its destination – London.

The Polish girl; that's all her identity had been, had a kind of mystery about her, a mystical inner quality that men would fall for. Her eyes, slightly wide-set, grey with flecks of green, were mesmeric.

Long after the delivery van had disappeared into the night, Ramsay was still watching for its tail lights, before he stirred himself and walked back to the house.

Fifty minutes into the flight, one of the crewmen crouched down from the cockpit and made his way to the doorway. Eva stood and he checked her parachute. Once satisfied, he gave her the thumbs-up. She looked back at Chainbridge, the man who had turned her life around and introduced her to de Witte and Brandt. He smiled, and gave her a cheery wave.

She took a deep breath and closed her eyes, trying to slow her heart down.

"leave her to the sharks....."

The crewman studied his watch. After what felt like an eternity, he pulled the door open and Eva plunged into the night.

Eva crept to the edge of the wood and in the intermittent moonlight, widened the roots of a tree with a telescopic shovel and buried her parachute. Pausing from time to time, fearful of German patrols, she listened intently over the rustling of the leaves in the night air. Her heart was still racing from the drop. Using the shovel's blade, she hacked some smaller overhead branches to cover the roots.

A twig snapped. She held her Mauser pistol at hip height and stared into the forest's murk. The faces of the young, intense and eager group appeared, led by a tall woman who coolly levelled a machine pistol at her.

"Password?"

"Chopin."

The woman smiled and lowered the gun.

"George Sand, welcome to France. My name is Mireille."

"Beautiful name, I'm Eva."

"Do you know in the old Gestapo files they called you 'The Spider'?"

Eva smiled.

"Nice to be appreciated. Shall we…?" Eva held up her pistol, palm up. After a moment, everyone put their guns away.

Mireille was olive-skinned with dark, deep Moroccan eyes beneath her heavy woollen hat; a beautiful woman too exotic to put onto a train to an extermination camp. The group all shook Eva's hand, one of the men, handsome, no more than nineteen grinned at her.

"Are all English ladies as beautiful as you?"

Mireille tut-tutted and glowered at him.

Eva smiled.

"They are. Here, take this." Eva threw the shovel to the boy, who caught it deftly and turned with a grin and the bow of a conjuror to his comrades.

"Make sure the Germans don't find it on you."

The boy's grin slipped. He placed it into the inside of his heavy, black lumber jacket.

"There's an abandoned farmhouse nearby. We'll prepare there," said Mireille and silently the five stepped into the forest as spotlights lit the night sky and the barking of dogs grew louder.

***

Aboard *Serenity*, Foucault studied Hitler's private physician, Theodor Morell. The flaccid, toad-like physician was wolfing down the silver service breakfast. His body odour drifted across the table, and his uniform appeared frayed and greasy.

"The Fürher?"

"He's well, very well and responding to treatment." Morell reached for another bread roll, his nails were grimed. Sitting opposite him, Bausch smiled thinly.

"That is excellent news, *'Herr Needle'*."

Morell ignored the jibe, mopping the last pieces of poached egg with the bread in precise swirls around the plate. Coffee was served by a liveried attendant who poured at arm's length, turning away from the stench.

Bausch felt uncomfortable amid the opulence of the ship, the voyage had been an indulgent cruise, nothing more. He had drunk in the extravagantly stocked bar, he had swum in the heated swimming pool, slept in a comfortable cabin with fresh sheets every day and had jogged every deck with the cold, unpleasant Hannah Wolfe who had rebuffed his advances. He preferred the Himmler's SS stud farms out in the eastern provinces where the next generation of the master race was being bred. The Aryan girls there were far more accommodating. In stony silence Bausch and Wolfe had exercised in the ship's gymnasium and dined like the Rockefellers by candle light at night.

What galled him most was he could be serving Hitler faithfully at Rastenburg, instead of where he was now; in exile. He had to find a way to 'work towards the Führer' again.

He reviled the doctor sitting in front of him, like a hog in a suit, never far from Hitler; always hovering about with his pills and potions.

"Here are the relevant documents in relation to the consignment for our dear Adolf."

Foucault slipped over a manila folder; it was a full inventory of drugs. Morell was flying to Rastenburg, to Hitler's eastern command to administer them to him personally.

"Also, my dear doctor, is a message. It's simple: England is bankrupt and my fellow lords and peers do not want to see the empire handed piece by piece over to America. Tell him it's a draft peace agreement. Tell The Fürher that we have fellow Americans who would be happy to see the back of Roosevelt," and putting

Stalin in the same place was just too tempting a target. "Please pass on our warmest wishes to Herr Hitler and wish him a speedy recovery on our behalf."

An attendant heaved the three-quarter length leather coat over the bulky doctor's frame, angling his head away from the smell as he did it. Morell gave a slovenly straight-armed salute and departed for the quayside, where a chauffeur driven car was waiting to take him to a Luftwaffe airbase. As he squeezed through the door, Hannah Wolfe appeared in the corridor. With her full curves and the corpulent apothecary passing her by with a lecherous grin, she did her best to press herself against the bulkhead, so no part of him would brush against her.

"Who is that schwein?" she asked as she nodded to the coffee pot. The attendant nearly fell over himself as he dashed to the table. To Foucault's delight, she was in a white top and trousers with high boots; she had been practicing the fencing moves he had taught her on the voyage.

"Hitler's personal physician."

Hannah's expression turned to genuine shock.

"Our Führer is unwell?"

A madman with rampant syphilis, thought Foucault.

"Nothing more than stress, I believe, Hannah."

On the breakfast table, an ornate telephone rang. Foucault answered. A private train, owned by the Gauleiter of Marseilles, Guy Michelet, was waiting to depart for Paris.

"Thank you."

He turned to Hannah.

"Fancy a weekend in Paris?"

SEVENTEEN
Paris

The motorcade swept from Luftwaffe Beauvais into Paris; Bormann's personal black Mercedes was flanked by SS motorcycle outriders who stopped at the intersections halting traffic, barking orders to the local gendarmerie. He brought Paris to a standstill. At Place de la Concorde at the junction of rue de Rivoli, Av Gabriel and the Champs Elysees stood the Hotel Crillon; the Nazi Occupation Headquarters. Bormann alighted and assisted his beautiful companion Marianne, out of the vehicle; they were ushered into the sumptuous building by an SS colour guard.

In his private quarters, he met Charles Foucault who appraised Bormann's companion as if she were a prize filly. She walked through the white panelled room with the high ceilings with the assured stride of youth. Foucault kissed her hand gallantly,

"Enchanted." He said.

"She's leaving." Said Bormann

The words seemed to cut her to the quick. She glided from the room.

"I keep the upper floors here for the Prix de l'Arc de Triomphe – good flight, Reichsleiter Bormann?" Foucault's German was flawless.

Bormann nodded.

"It was adequate."

Foucault looked around the room, before the war he had toured Paris with Edward VIII and Wallis Simpson and stayed in this very suite. Someone like Bormann would have been carrying their cases, now he was the second most powerful man in Europe. He twisted the ring with the in-set molar around his finger.

"Have you availed of the barbershop here?" he asked.

"No." said Bormann

"Wonderful service. The American delegation had it installed here during the Versailles peace conference." Said Foucault, "I had a shave here, first one I'd had in three years."

He paused to see if the remark had had any effect – Bormann seemed untouched by the Versailles Treaty.

"At least the elevators are working better." Said Foucault.

Bormann handed Foucault a chit; stamped by the Reichsbank it had details of a gold transaction placed in Foucault's Swiss bank account.

" *Thor's Hammer'* is to proceed," as he spoke, he produced reams of files and papers and stacked them on the delicate ornate desk. Foucault's thoughts turned to the beautiful girl, maybe he could lever her away from the dour bureaucrat.

"Excellent. As your agents have confirmed in Argentina; Roosevelt has given instruction he has to set sail from America. It's either Cairo or Tehran, knowing Stalin is paranoid about travel, he won't venture further than those sites. Did the communique with the co-ordinates arrive?"

Bormann nodded as he poured generous Brandies for both of them.

"Can you ship the components directly to SS Crimea?"

"We're not expecting any more Royal Navy intercepts, I've made sure through the admiralty; both the *Aurora* and *Serenity* have been cleared through Gibraltar."

He had several close companions at King George's court and Whitehall keeping him appraised.

"Viktor Bausch?"

"He's remained on in Marseilles, he's been excellent company."

"Guy Michelet?"

"His reach exceeded his grasp; I made sure he suffered a huge loss in Buenos Aires."

"He's still faithful to the cause, but yes, turn the screw tighter at every opportunity."

Bormann opened a dossier; the hour-glass shape of Hannah Wolfe sprang out of the photograph beside her personal file.

"Officer Wolfe?"

"Here in Paris with me; she's in the suite above."

"I'll speak with her later in private."

"I have placed your own private shipments at my stud *Casa Rosa*, have you any more items you wish to store there?"

Bormann had shipped priceless artworks, plundered gold and a substantial amount of US dollars. No doubt his mammoth JU390 was being loaded up again.

"Nothing more for now, thank you, Herr Foucault." Foucault smarted at the tone of the response; he wasn't used to being addressed in this manner by a low-born.

"It's a pity Bausch will miss the ceremony." Foucault felt a sudden moment of exhaustion, reaching into his pocket; he produced a gold foil wrap packet. Opening it, he poured a line of powder along the back of his hand and snorted it up.

"One of Dr. Morell's little pick-me-ups," he offered the packet to Bormann.

"Let's get on with this." Said Bormann.

They descended in an elevator to the basement. At the doorway they were met by two Waffen SS officers in full dress uniform. They handed Foucault and Bormann two black full-length silk robes, with large cowls. A small corridor lit by wall-mounted flambeaus led to a wooden door, inlaid with swastikas and ancient runes. Foucault's eyes adjusted to the gloom.

On the other side of the door was a room, painted completely black. This, too, was lit by twelve flambeaus positioned along the walls. The room was circular and inlaid into the floor with the finest Italian marble was the Sonnenrad. At each of the conjoining points were robed figures, their features hidden. Ten of the points were occupied, two remained. Foucault and Bormann took their place on the circle.

Obergruppenführer Kurt Dietrich Hoeberichts draped in a robe of the blackest silk, entered from a concealed door. He wore a Nepalese headdress, a pointed helmet of pure silver with a long flowing horsetail of vermillion. The effect of Morell's powder gave Foucault a huge surge of well-being as Hoeberichts began swinging a polished silver incense burner. The others began a deep groaning chant. Hoeberichts stopped at every point along the circle, standing before each figure and the chant increased. Once he had done a circuit, the scarecrow-like Obergruppenführer went to the centre of the circle. He placed the incense burner down and clapped loudly seven times. The chant stopped. The door opened and Marianne stepped out, naked except for a pure white diaphanous shroud; her youthful flesh glowed in the flickering light.

"This maid, Marianne, is twelfth generation Aryan, her line goes directly back to the Teutonic Knights and back to The Battle of Grunwald where her ancestor fell heroically defending the order and the German nation against the untermensch Poles."

Foucault looked at the beautiful brunette, she reminded him of the spy Eva Molenaar; he wondered idly if the sharks had got her.

He found the idea arousing.

"With her blood, we will consecrate *Thor's Hammer*."

Hoeberichts produced a long silver knife; festooned is precious stones. He took Marianne's arm and made a small incision in the forearm. Once the blood began to flow, he gathered it in an ornate silver phial. Once it was full, he held it aloft and the chant began again, increasing in volume. Marianne joined in, her voice, faint and reedy; no doubt under the influence of a narcotic. Foucault found himself humming along, his body thrilling to the ceremony; it took him to a place of euphoria, something appeared in his peripheral vision, he looked up. Two hooded men came through the door and stood either side of Marianne. They tenderly guided her back through the door.

"The weapon is to be consecrated with this pure Aryan blood. It will be poured onto the first shell. Heil Hitler."

"Heil Hitler."

The chant rose to a frenzied scream, twelve right arms outstretched in salute, twelve voices chanting Hitler's name and the officiator raised his arms and screamed:

"Another thousand years!"

And Charles Foucault believed it to be so.

"Amen," he whispered.

EIGHTEEN
Marseilles

Eklund watched the harbour appear with a sense of relief; despite continuous searches of the ship, oiler, unlicensed rating, Paul Hauk was missing; presumed dead. A sense of pall had descended once the Japanese had discovered Nagasawa's body. They went about their duties with due diligence and, though Eklund couldn't be sure, with a degree of uncertainty enlisted men had when a leader was dead. Jongbloed reported to Eklund and his officers that Hauk had simply 'snapped' and had probably thrown himself overboard.

"This stuff," he had waved his moonshine around, "drives you crazy. He kept talking about suicide after the slaughter."

His moonshine had been thrown overboard, and the Japanese first officer had taken over running engineering, keeping a watchful eye on the South African. The U-boats had guided the ship along with the harbour pilot into a secluded berth at La Joliette. A fleet of trucks with armoured escort arrived to take the huge containers off the vessel. The enormous Bakelite tubes were to remain on board and offloaded in the Crimea. The Japanese in full Imperial Navy fatigues, filed down to the gangplank and boarded the last truck. Once the containers had been lifted and carefully inspected by one of the truck drivers before being loaded, the armed convoy sped off with several police cars leading the way.

Brandt was frozen to the bone. His beard was tangled and stiff with salt from the sea, his heavy woollen hat, his greatcoat and two jumpers, soaked. He checked his watch; it was 2am.

Finding a gap between the Bakelite tubes, he had wrapped himself in a heavy tarpaulin and lay looking up at the stars. Peeking out of the tarpaulin, he spied two Japanese patrolling the deck. Instinctively, he flattened himself down. He pulled Carrington's knife from his heavy coat. The Japanese gave the ropes securing the tubes and good tug. If everything had come loose, the three of them would be crushed, thought Brandt. The Japanese ambled away, their voices carried by the wind.

Once the dawn had begun to creep across the sky, he eased himself off the tubes and made his way aft. The decks were silent and unlit. Paying out the ropes and checking the knots, he leapt over the side.

He had been hanging from the vessel's aft section, secured with a series of secure knots. Once the harbour wall had passed, he began to lower himself incrementally down as the engines slowed. As the ship's mooring lines were thrown over, Brandt began to swing himself forward and back until he had the momentum of a pendulum. At the very last swing, he released the last of his holding knots and landed neatly on the docks of Marseilles. Amid the bustle of the dockers, trucks and cranes preparing to unload *The Aurora*, he hoped that the safe house had a bath.

He walked; his steps unsteady for the first few minutes as his muscles adapted to solid ground again. Intermittent showers added to the city's gloom. The buildings in the lower section of the labyrinthine alleys appeared to have been expertly dynamited and the rubble left strewn across the streets. The safe house was miraculously intact. Brandt checked the door's number, and then brought out the Nambu. He prayed the Japanese pistol hadn't been damaged with salt water. He knocked.

A man stepped from the shadows of the doorway behind him. Brandt closed his eyes in exhaustion and desperation as the muzzle of a revolver was pressed against the back of his head.

"Captain Nicklaus Brandt, AOK Norwegen-Alpine Korps?"

Brandt whispered the code word.

"*I'm going so far…*"

"*..it'll take a dollar to send me a postcard.*"

"Your German is flawless as usual, Henry." For the first time in twenty-two days, Brandt began to relax. Henry glowered from beneath his trilby, as he put his gun away.

"And you, of all people, should know that you never drop your guard. You look like the wreck of the Hesperus, Nick. I didn't recognise you and you're not as tall as Carrington."

"I'll take your word for it. Carrington didn't make it."

Henry nodded ruefully. He knocked at the door in a series of raps. It opened and Brandt felt an overwhelming sense of relief as his old friend, Sergeant Erik Kant, stood in the doorway. Glancing up and down the deserted street, he nodded for the men to enter.

"Good to see you, sir."

"Kant, tell me there's a bed and coffee?"

Inside, the main living room had a basic army cot, but this was compensated with heavy blankets. Brandt shook Erik Kant's hand warmly, then began easing off his water-logged clothes.

"The whole area was dynamited by the German army, there's a sink with water," said Chainbridge, "there's a small water supply."

Kant handed Brandt a piping hot cup of coffee.

Brandt slumped onto the cot, he felt every day of his thirty-four years.

"The barrels I saw in the dry dock were hung under the ship's keel."

Chainbridge went into the corner of the room; there was a radio transmitter and he began to talk into it, sending a coded phrase.

Brandt was exhausted; he decided he'd wash in the morning. The coffee's heat went straight into his bones, his muscles ached and his feet were the texture of marinated meat from the saltwater and from walking in heavy boots. He stretched out on the cot and wondered if Jongbloed had survived.

He glanced up at Kant.

"Olga?"

The lupine, lanky sergeant grinned.

"She's well, sir, gave us all a fright, but she made it out of Germany in one piece."

"She's still hitched to you? Her sense of humour's developing. Hauptman, Bader, Kramer?"

"We're all here, sir."

Brandt looked at Chainbridge,

"Nick, we're going to blow a few things up," he said. The transmitter crackled back and Chainbridge responded.

"Excellent," said Brandt.

Then he fell asleep.

NINETEEN
The Chateau Rimbaud, Marseilles

Mathilde flitted and dived above the immaculately manicured lawns of the chateau, revelling in the freedom of the lazy thermals. A young peregrine falcon, she was fast and sleek like an arrow. Ascending into the heavens, she hovered, poised with lethal intent, before she spied the proffered treat. She swooped silently onto the gauntlet and tenderly took the lure in her beak.

"I think she likes you," said the Gauleiter of Marseilles, Guy Michelet. He was dressed in an open-necked shirt, pleated slacks and patent leather shoes. He smoked a cigarillo in a delicate manner, watching his prized falcon as a father would his favourite child.

"She's beautiful, Monsieur Michelet," replied Eva.

Mathilde allowed Eva to fasten the Alymeri jesses to her legs, the long strips of leather delicately secured around her razor talons. Behind them, from the chateau's open doors, conversation, music and laughter floated over the gardens and verdant maze that shimmered in the early morning s un.

Michelet watched the beautiful woman stroke the falcon's downy feathers. Mathilde responded by dancing daintily on the leather gauntlet, the bells on her jesses tinkling softly. With a shrill cry, she allowed Eva to secure the soft leather Dutch hood over her head. The hood looked antique; bejewelled with delicate sapphires and rubies in the shape of arabesques; North African in origin, she thought. She handed the falcon gently back to Michelet.

His eyes took in Eva's figure; tall, elegant, shapely, and dressed in the black sequined evening gown that tapered down to the calf, suggesting long legs and revealing delicate ankles. The heavy leather gauntlet made her look like a buccaneer, he thought.

They had met in the Hotel La Canebière in Marseilles the night before, where a party had been organised for the local Nazi officials and high ranking Wehrmacht, SS and U-boat officers on leave. Michelet owned the hotel and had closed it to guests for the weekend-long soiree. As a Gauleiter he was the unquestioned ruler in his region.

The party had a number of local and Parisian girls attending there; each wore a silk ribbon around their arm; red for sexual favours, yellow for hostesses and white for women exclusive to the highest ranking men, at the highest price.

"May I ask your name?" he enquired.

"Helene," Eva replied, she never told Michelet her last name. He liked it like that, enjoying the company of a cool, beautiful, anonymous woman. Her accent, he thought, was Northern, Calais, possibly.

"Do you know Marseilles?"

"I do, I lived here before the war, in the Arab Quarter just off La Canebiere. I lived with an artist, does that shock you?"

Michelet smiled, she was direct, confident and assured; a real challenge.

"Not at all Helene, may I ask what happened to your artist?"

Eva had met Theo Kassinski in Krakow, became his muse and travelled with him to France. Theo had returned to Poland before the war.

And she had joined British Intelligence.

"He left to go back home."

"And where was home?"

"New York." She said.

She assumed Theo was dead now; because he was Polish and he was Jewish.

"And what is Helene's tale, after that?"

"I'll have another glass of wine please, monsieur Michelet."

Her breath was warm on his cheek. The faint scent of wine, tobacco and perfume mingling together entranced him. When she removed the white ribbon from her wrist and handed it to him, his heart had skipped a beat. Helene...

Then, on a whim, the suave Michelet had decided to continue the party back at his Chateau.

A convoy of luxury and high-performance cars raced through the dawn, laden with champagne, brandy and the hotel's finest fare to Chateau Rimbaud. Surrounded by a high wall and lush woods, it flew the Vichy flag: Marshal Pétain's standard; the tricolour with the double-headed axe. Alongside it, the swastika hung from its medieval turrets. The cars swept into the forecourt and Eva observed the gatehouse at the front, the unused stables, and the imposing Cour d'honneur entrance. She committed everything she saw to memory, including the names of all the Vichy and German officers as they made their way through the cold reception to the main dining room. The last car to arrive was a Bugatti 64, jet black, growling into the driveway. From it, alighted Viktor Bausch, haughty in full SS uniform. He strode to the passenger door and assisted one of the girls from the party.

A gramophone was cranked up and lusty Parisian show tunes filled the room. Taking a place on the leather lounge; Bausch produced a small box of chocolates from his jet black tunic pocket with a flourish,

"Panzerscholade, ladies and gentlemen!!" German tank crew amphetamine used to stave off fatigue. He downed a few in one go, then, he forced one into the mouth of the pretty blonde with a glass of champagne. He jeered her discomfiture.

Bausch had yet to recognise Eva. Either he was stupid, or women had no relevance to him, she thought. Peripheral pleasures.

The box went around and Eva palmed one pretending to chew. Michelet took one and swallowed it down with a heavy Burgundy.

Then some of the couples cleared the rugs and furniture recklessly to create an impromptu dance floor. The windows and doors were opened and the remaining guests stepped onto the terrace to watch the breath-taking sunrise, then one, by one, they disappeared into the many bedrooms, leaving Michelet and Eva alone.

"You are a very beautiful woman, Helene, I'd like to introduce you to another beautiful creature; Mathilde."

"Thank you, Monsieur." Eva studied him; he was over six feet tall, tanned, well-groomed, mid-forties, smooth and urbane; a career Nazi; a man who liked dressing up.

"Have you always lived here?"

Michelet grinned.

"My family can trace their lineage back to the reign of King Phillip the first and took the first Crusade. My blood is steeped in these stones. You don't look sleepy, my darling Helene, do you ever sleep?"

"Never," her smile captivated him, full lips that were framed by dimples, suggested exquisite pleasure without even trying. He wanted to kiss her there and then, just to taste her.

"Shall we retire for an hour or two?"

Michelet's heartbeat quickened. Linking arms, they strolled back through the well-swept weathering yard, to Mathilde's mews. Carefully Michelet placed her on her perch inside the mews and removed the hood. After closing the door over gently, they turned back toward the main building.

TWENTY
Berlin

Hannah Wolfe had flown in from Paris. As she descended the aircrafts steps she could see heavy construction under way around Berlin Templehof airport. Heavy gun emplacements were being built into the arc of the complex. Military personnel were running drills. Sappers and engineers worked through the cold.

Her meeting with Bormann in her sumptuous quarters in Hotel Crillon had been brief.

"I want you to return to Argentina. *'Casa Rosa'*, Foucault's stud. An American senator has made himself at home there. A preacher."

"Pastor, man of God?" she asked,

"An inconvenience." Replied Bormann.

"My duty is to the Reich. My superiors?"

"Have been notified. You are to report to Abwehr Berlin. You are to inform Herr Malleus that you have been reassigned."

"I answer to Himmler."

"You answer to me from now on." Said Bormann.

Bormann noted she had had a busy shopping day; stacks of boxes stood in the corner of the room. He knew she was wealthy and knew how she had acquired her wealth.

"This operation is for the Reich, Scharführer Wolfe. If we are pushed back by the reds, we need a fall-back position. The British have Canada; we must explore this option with a friendly country overseas. There are none in Europe."

"We are winning in the east." She said.

Bormann didn't like to be interrupted,

"He likes blondes, young blondes. You will have a unit at your disposal."

"You want this American removed?"

"Accidentally; you have a knack. *Casa Rosa* must be taken. Foucault has private guachos and the American, his congregation. He's building a revival down there."

Bormann looked up at the pneumatic liaison.

"We must find somewhere to continue this vision. Hitler promised us a thousand years. It is our duty to give him that."

"A thousand years, Reichsleiter." Replied Hannah

"And, Hannah."

"Yes?"

"Kill all the horses there."

"As you wish, Reichsleiter."

Outside Berlin Templehof, an official Mercedes Benz was waiting for her. The liveried Kreigsmarine driver saluted her. She was ushered through the non-descript halls of Abwehr HQ offices into the offices of Department IIIF and Section Chief, Hermann Malleus.

"Scharführer Wolfe."

"Herr Oberst, Malleus."

"Please take a seat. Good flight?"

"Uneventful."

"Have you your accommodation arranged?"

"I keep a room at The Kaiserhof. I will be staying there tonight."

"Coffee?"

"No thank you."

His hand hovered over his intercom.

"You have no objection?"

"No, by all means."

He requested two coffees.

"In case you change your mind. I've recently discovered a South American blend."

"Thank you, Herr Oberst. But I did say no."

Malleus shrugged. On his desk was her dossier, he had been reading it before she arrived.

"Congratulations on your recent mission. You helped deliver the critical components for *'Thor's Hammer'* intact and eliminated an Allied agent."

"For the second time. She drowned."

"For the second time. Did you see her drown?"

"There were sharks, Herr Oberst."

Malleus was urbane and groomed. His suits were Parisian, his cigarettes, American. He was a little greyer than the last time she had met him. She also knew he was under suspicion with the SS; Himmler had been building a dossier not only on him, but his superior Admiral Canaris.

Malleus studied the young officer. Out of her SS uniform she was equally impressive.

"I have received your transfer papers from SS Hauptamt - Bormann wants you to clean up a little problem of his making?"

"It's my duty to the Reich."

"I've alerted Buenos Aires station. We have arranged a modest dwelling for you and your squad. With the war stretching manpower resources, it seems Herr Bormann has resorted to recruiting from the prison system."

"I can look after myself."

"I don't doubt it for a minute. Your travel permits. Currency."

She folded them away.

"Thank you."

Without invitation, she took a cigarette from the ornate box on his desk and lit it with his service lighter.

The coffees arrived, served by a man in navy uniform.

"What happened to that Spanish secretary of yours?" she asked. Her cold blue eyes had narrowed; either from the cigarette smoke or a calculated thought.

"Transferred out." Malleus replied.

He was conscious of Miss Wolfe's sudden ascent.

"Unfortunate," she replied, "Almost as unfortunate as the captured spy de Witte escaping."

She let the comment hang, enjoying Malleus's discomfiture.

"We gleaned nothing new, but yes, an unfortunate event."

"You should have killed him then." She replied.

"We aren't all savages like Himmler." He said.

"An unfortunate statement, Herr Oberst." She replied. Malleus stirred the coffee with slow deliberation. An icy trickle of sweat burrowed its way down his spine. He noticed a slight tremble in his hand as he placed the spoon on the edge of the tiny saucer.

"You will at least this time, Hannah, be travelling in comfort." He said.

"Comfort, Herr Oberst?"

"Herr Bormann must be sweating about his plunder; he's chartered an airship. You depart 20.00hrs tomorrow night."

"I have already received my orders, Herr Oberst."

"To tidy up Bormann's little problem?"

Hannah paused, she smiled slightly as she exhaled her cigarette smoke.

"Our final redoubt, Herr Oberst."

Malleus opened a drawer on his uncluttered, orderly desk. He produced a manila file.

"Before you depart, here's some reading material you might enjoy; for the last three years, there has been a search for a renegade unit of German soldiers working for Churchill."

Hannah opened the file on her lap.

Her perfume was just a shade too strong, thought Malleus, a tad too sweet; stamping her scent for attention.

"Nicklaus Brandt, Captain, AOK Norwegen-Alpine Korps; the mountain regiment charged with capturing Lenin's mausoleum and once achieving their objective, were subsequently liquidated by the SS."

Not a handsome man, Brandt, thought Hannah, but a steady gaze and strong mouth, his skin shaped and lined by the outdoors.

Her gaze flicked to the pale bureaucrat in front of her.

"Mountaineer, part-time skiing instructor after failing to get a place in the Olympics; thought to be a political decision – refused to take the oath. Iron cross, Knight's cross for action on the Russian front, the good Captain likes to do things the hard way." Said Malleus.

Hannah flicked through the other dossiers as Malleus spoke.

"Staff sergeant Kant, Erik; Brandt's right hand man, Kramer, Jan; Bader, Hans; Hauptmann, Rudolf – all AOK Norwegen-Alpine, highly trained in mountaineering, explosives and special operations and all decorated for bravery before being killed with their captain Brandt. Now all alive and well in France at this very moment. They also have a female cohort accompanying them, a real killer. We don't know her identity, but our intelligence suggests she was operating here in Germany and recently crossed the border into France to meet up with Brandt and his men. Perhaps, your boss,

Himmler was too quick to indicate they had been eliminated in Russia?"

Hannah held up the last photo,

"That's the agent we fed to the sharks; her name was Sheridan - codename 'The Spider'? The one I indicated to you was operating in Italy last year and you duly ignored? Very dramatic title by the way, Herr Malleus."

"Her Allied codename is 'Chopin'. Her real name is Eva, last name not entirely clear. We believe she's Polish, started as a courier for MI6 before the war, but know moved on to allied intelligence. Henning was one of her recent surnames. She's in France as well with this team – are you sure you saw her drown?"

Hannah paused.

Inwardly she cursed at herself for not killing Eva in the room, only that Foucault and Bausch had prised them apart.

"Yes. Before you go to Argentina to tidy up Bormann's mess, perhaps you might want to look at tidying up this loose end? Your liaison in France is included at the back. "

Hannah methodically dropped her cigarette into Malleus' coffee cup.

"I'll make arrangements tonight."

"Might be a good idea to cancel your flight to Argentina, Wolfe?"

He watched her stride out of the room.

Her perfume remained like a faint sneer.

He kept a copy of the dossiers and ran his finger down through them – highly capable men and a woman sniper all fighting for the other side.

Men and a woman capable of causing real problems and slipping back into the shadows after the damage was done.

He lit another cigarette and stretched out his leg. Kneading the wasted muscle beneath his trousers; the surgeons had managed to save his leg at Verdun in 1917, he dialled his secretary.

"Get me Headquarters in Paris."

TWENTY-ONE
Marseilles

Henry Chainbridge lowered his binoculars and glanced over at Brandt, Erik Kant and Rudy Hauptman,

"Japanese sentries, armed."

"They were on the ship," said Brandt watching them through his sniper sight.

"We're at the right address then," said Hauptman, a tall, wiry man, his shaved head covered by a thick woollen hat. He took a piece of Swedish tobacco and placed it behind his upper back molar, then adjusted the sights on his rifle. They had travelled over two days from Switzerland, with incendiaries and weapons supplied through the British mission in Berne.

"A long walk up," said Kant. He took a piece of proffered tobacco.

Deeper into the wood, armed with heavy machine guns and a wide-band radio were Hans Bader and Jan Kramer, watching the road for passing Vichy and German army patrols.

"Olga?" asked Brandt

"Inside," replied Chainbridge. He inhaled deeply, the air mixed with the verdant scents.

The Chateau appeared deserted, the only indication of anyone there was the loud music drifting across the grounds.

"What about local resistance?" asked Brandt.

"SOE smoothed the way for us. They'll stay out of the way," replied Chainbridge. Spread out before him was a map of the area. "That, of course, means we're on our own if we get into trouble."

"A lot of back roads," said Brandt.

Kant and Hauptman inched over through the undergrowth, the four men pored over the map.

"The materials were shipped in by truck, so it'll be coming back to the port," said Chainbridge.

"If they haven't shipped already. Be easier to hit the truck," said Kant.

"Depends on its escort," said Hauptman. He scanned the Chateau with his binoculars. He paused.

"Your girlfriend, Kant."

From a downstairs window, a small light appeared and began flashing Morse code.

It was Olga Mirinova.

***

Michelet stretched out on his huge bed, trembling with anticipation. Every caress of Eva's sent electrical surges through his nervous system.

"You will have to trust me," she whispered.

The bedroom was panelled in dark, aged oak and heavy drapes. On the bedside cabinet was a brandy decanter and crystal glasses. Removing her stockings and allowing Michelet a view of her long legs and suspenders, she wrapped the stockings around his wrists and fastened them securely to the headboard. Once tethered, she ran her nails along his chest.

He arched his back.

She straddled his chest, her skirt riding up her thighs, Michelet's heart rate accelerated as he looked up at her, the folds of the gown stopping at the top of her creamy white thighs. She leaned over and poured two generous measures of cognac. Grinning impishly, she placed the glass on Michelet's lips and allowed him to sip. The rich liquid flowed down his throat. The sunlight danced through the drapes, catching Eva's flesh on the arms and shoulders; she was incredibly beautiful. Her weight on his chest aroused him intently. She offered him another sip, using her knees to push his shoulders deeper into the mattress.

It was then that he noticed she had a paper towel scrunched up in her hand. In one swift movement Eva stuffed the Panzerscholade into his mouth, followed by a hefty slug of brandy. Michelet felt the amphetamine surge through his system, bringing him to a state of euphoria.

"Your keys?"

He felt Eva's breath on his throat.

"In my bathroom, my darling Helene," he replied.

Her face and hair shimmered and her voice seemed light and distant. His heart rate was racing; he began to sweat.

"Your gun?" her lips on his throat, added to the joyous sensation coursing through his veins.

"Bedside dresser."

"Good boy."

She forced another glass of brandy down his throat. It burned his cheeks as it spilled. He tried to struggle.

Keeping her weight on him, she opened the top drawer. Feeling around, her fingers found a leather case. The size of a cigar box, inside was a pearl-handled Mauser parabellum pistol, pristine in the crimson velvet lining. She checked the weapon's breech and released the safety.

"One more question, my love. How do I access your cellars?"

"Below the main stairs, the door on the left."

He began planting kisses on her legs, his neck straining like a tortoise. She clubbed him with the gun. Grinning, he passed out. She climbed off him and went to his bathroom. She found the keys, a thick ring of various sizes with hand-written tags on them. Obviously Gauleiter Guy Michelet, beneath all the panache, was a forgetful man.

Eva closed the bedroom door behind her and padded down the corridor. The rooms along the corridor resounded to orgies happening behind the solid oak doors. On the far side of the passageway, Eva heard a film blaring, it sounded like a car was racing and a woman was screaming with pleasure at the same time.

It was in the corridor below that she found Bausch. She could hear a woman sobbing, screaming suddenly then begging for her life. The sound of furniture breaking was then followed by an eerie silence. Eva found the door where the noise had come from and tried the handle. It opened quietly. She raised the pistol and eased her way in. Bausch had his back to her. He was naked, standing over the blonde who was lying prone, face down. He was oddly hairless; smooth like a statue. A small table lay in pieces around her. With deliberate movements, he reached down for one of the table legs and raised it over his head.

"Put it down."

Bausch turned slowly. He was heavily muscled and sweating from his exertions. He was unsteady on his feet, his eyes red and glazed. Eva could see the champagne bottle on the floor and the bed clothes strewn across the floor. Blood was pooling around the girl's head on the floor.

"Okay, pretty. Don't shoot," he said.

Eva stepped into the room.

"Remember me?"

"Should I?" he blinked a few times, his gaze was glassy.

"We've met before." Said Eva.

"I don't recall."

"Is she dead?"

Bausch gripped the table leg tighter. His forearm muscles were contorted with the effort.

"Hopefully."

Overhead, something collapsed violently, it sounded like a bed or wardrobe being broken. Laughter and cheers followed. There was another loud crash, it sounded like a bed collapsing, followed by more laughter.

Eva fired twice.

Viktor Bausch collapsed, staring blankly at the holes in his chest. He dropped the chair leg, his hands then suddenly fluttered outwards, his fingers clasping the air. Glass or porcelain shattered in the room above. Eva went over to the girl, she rolled her over. The girls face was bloodied and bruised. Her breathing was coming in short gasps, her eye lids swollen slits. Eva helped her up and brought her over to the bed.

Bausch refused to die and began crawling toward the door, leaving a viscous trail of blood. There was a loud shot from the corridor outside; the bullet prising his shaved head apart and he lay still. The maid who walked into the room, carrying a pistol nodded at Eva and checked Bausch's pulse.

"Eva."

"Olga."

"This place is going to go up like a roman candle."

"This girl needs a doctor."

"No time and besides, she shouldn't be bedding the Waffen SS."

164

The dark eyed Chechen came over to Eva. She was brusque and coiled in her movements.

They had met once before on the Russian front; part of a rag tag group trying to stop Lenin's corpse leaving the USSR.

"Has he a car?" she nodded to Bausch.

The two women searched the room. Along with the Bugatti's keys, they found another Luger and a crocodile skin attaché case. Eva went back to the girl.

"We can't leave her like this," she hoisted the girl up. "Help me."

Olga stared coldly, then with a grunt, helped Eva.

"There's a small lodge near the aviary. We'll put her there."

The corridors of the Chateau had become quiet; the party-goers sleeping off their excesses, a cracked record was stuck on an aria, it skipped, juddered and wailed in one of the bedrooms. Olga and Eva took the semi-conscious girl down the main staircase and out into the courtyard at the back. On the green near the wall, lay a man's body.

"There are armed Japanese in the building."

They found the small lodge and placed the girl there. She was still unconscious. They rolled her over onto her front. Eva went to the aviary and opened the locks; if the building was going to burn, she wanted Mathilde and the other birds to have an escape route. Eva jammed the gate open.

"I've the keys to the cellar."

"I know where it is."

They came to the doorway, it was open. They went down the stairs, lit only by the light coming through the door and came to a huge, wheel-lock metal door, open slightly ajar. A light was on inside. Just inside the door lay two dead Japanese men, shot. Eva and Olga pressed themselves against the metal door. Olga let out a low, deep whistle. They held their breaths for a moment. A low whistle emanated and from behind the door, Erik Kant's face appeared in the doorway. He grinned.

"Wait 'til you see this, ladies."

The cellars had been excavated into the Chateau's ancient foundations. On the ground floor level, banks of consoles stood in a line with electrical switches and levers. On the far side of the metallic pit, Eva spotted Brandt.

"Well, well, well.," he said. He looked thin and tired, but his eyes were beautiful.

"Small world," she replied.

He tried to walk coolly toward her, but it turned into a loping dash.

He pulled Eva close to him, her fingers touched his face. She traced every line along it, dawdling on the roughly shaved stubble around his chin.

"I'm going to have to do something about that." She grinned.

They kissed deeply, tenderly, briefly.

Hauptman was on the radio transmitter, carefully tuning through the bandwidths.

Bader was leafing through sheaves of notes. He stopped.

"Herr, Chainbridge."

He held out a page.

"Bloody hell." said Chainbridge.

Brandt and Eva's moment was broken by the line of figures rushing past, Kant, Kramer, Olga, Hauptman and Bader.

Descending a metal stairwell and inching along a well-lit tunnel, they found huge steel vault doors. Brandt and Chainbridge heaved on the huge wheel and the doors slid grudgingly open. Beyond was a warren of a laboratory offices and desks and a fully operational electrical station.

"All the desks have been cleared," said Hauptman, "Drawers appear locked too."

"See if these are any use," said Eva tossing over the keys.

Hauptman was methodical as he tried the keys in every desk.

"No. Plan B."

He prised every one of the drawers open with a bayonet. Splinters and curses flew.

Olga and Kant took point. They crouched low on either side of the door for the cellar. Somewhere in the chateau, an alarm bell began ringing.

"We may have company," said Kant.

He threw the bag of incendiaries over to Chainbridge.

Bader and Kramer kicked over desks, dragging them into the centre of the room, making a crude barricade.

"We'll be fish in a barrel," muttered Kramer.

As Eva, Brandt and Chainbridge made their way deeper into the complex they came across an immense machine.

"It's a gas centrifuge," said Chainbridge.

"A what?" whispered Brandt.

"Bracken thought it was situated in somewhere outside Berlin, but obviously not," said Chainbridge, "It's a crude refinery, for want of a better word, Nick, but effective nonetheless. All they need is twenty kilos of fissile material to destroy a city. A city the size of Berlin."

The very air about them felt toxic.

"Loaded onto a bomb, a rocket," said Brandt.

"Or an artillery shell, Nick," said Chainbridge.

"Is it a good idea to blow this thing up, Henry?" said Eva.

"We don't have a choice," said Chainbridge.

"Eva's right, if we don't know what it can do, can we just wreck it?" said Brandt.

They froze as machine gun fire burst out behind them in the offices and stairwell beyond.

"I'm not going to waste good explosives on this, the walls must be feet thick," said Brandt.

He turned around and Eva was already back in the offices, firing.

Brandt and Chainbridge followed her. Bullets pinged and whistled, forcing them to crouch.

"All clear," shouted Hauptman.

Two more Japanese lay dead. The room was filled with smoke and the aftertaste of cordite.

"Think that's it," said Kramer. He was still crouching behind a desk.

They closed off the heavy doors to the centrifuge.

"I'll set the charges," said Hauptman.

"Time to leave," said Brandt.

"We have just a little over five minutes," said Chainbridge.

"I'll drive," said Eva.

Eva drove the Bugatti with Brandt and Chainbridge in it. Hauptman, Kramer, Bader and Olga followed behind them in one of the guests stolen Mercedes Benz. They made it to the rendezvous point at edge of the woods when the all the incendiaries exploded. The two cars pulled in and they watched the blazing chateau through binoculars. Kant, Hauptman and Brandt retrieved the buried equipment from the woods and loaded them into the boot of the Mercedes. The Chateau belched flames through every window, door and opening. A thick pall of smoke drifted across the blue skies and up toward the clouds. The Vichy and Nazi flags ignited in the super-heated air, and from within the building the screams began to drift on the wind.

"The Japs didn't put up much of a fight," said Brandt.

"There could still be more trapped in the chateau," said Chainbridge, he found the damp ground working its way into his knees. "There were a lot of heavy tyre tracks around the front and back driveways."

For the first time in a month Brandt allowed himself a fourth cigarette. The lupine sergeant Kant seemed to have an endless supply.

"It's a reasonable assumption then that the Japanese and the fissile materials are heading back to Marseilles, back to the gun's components," said Brandt.

"Back to the port?" asked Chainbridge.

"Back to that ship I was on.," said Brand, "..And, I know where it's moored."

"Looks like some people are getting out of the chateau," said Chainbridge.

In the intense blaze, sheets were being tossed out from the upper windows of the Chateau, naked men and partially clad women were lowering themselves down. A secondary explosion lifted a large section of the roof skyward and fragments of roof tile fell close to the edge of the woods.

Some of the people fell to earth in flames.

Brandt motioned to Kant and Hauptman.

"We're not done yet. Kant, Hauptmann; munitions status?" He said.

Hauptman looked out through the wooded glade as he made a mental inventory.

"Three incendiary timers left, about a half-kilo of plastic explosive and we have enough guns and ammunition for a limited operation, all-in-all if we're careful, about a half-hour tops."

Kant's expression was the same as Hauptman's – *be very, very cautious*.

"Enough explosives here to sink a ship?" Chainbridge asked.

Hauptman rubbed his chin, the explosives expert pondered for a moment.

"The type of ship Captain Brandt was on? No. Hull's too thick."

"Enough to damage the engine room or the ships propulsion, then?" asked Brandt.

"I don't have any waterproof timers, if we place everything we have in the engine room, then yes, we could do a lot of damage. Cripple her maybe, sink her no. Slow her down for a couple of days is the best we could do, Captain, Herr Chainbridge."

"The gun parts would need to be transferred then," said Brandt.

"If they haven't been offloaded already. Pity we can't sink her," said Chainbridge.

"Eklund, the captain had her running at maximum speed for the whole voyage, which means he was on a deadline. Crippling the ship might screw up that deadline by a day or so," said Brandt. He turned to Chainbridge,

"Small steps, to trip Hitler and his brown-shirt goons up, Henry."

"It's the ship's engine room, then," said Chainbridge.

"It'll be heavily guarded," said Kant.

"I think, I can get us aboard," said Eva.

Another explosion shook the ground. From their binoculars, Chateau Rimbaud's west wing crumpled down, leaving a pall of dust and smoke.

"That should bury the centrifuge." Said Chainbridge.

***

The *Aurora* lay silent at her moorings. Eva drove the Bugatti down the quayside and halted at the gangplank. The sun was beginning to set, drenching Marseilles in a deep orange across the city and giving the ocean a thicker texture as it lapped around the vessel. The two Japanese guards, brandishing machine guns looked in at her. Beside her sat Olga.

"We're expected aboard," grinned Eva.

She leaned over to one for the guards, allowing her cleavage to appear through the opening in her jacket. She handed him a piece of headed stationery from the Hotel La Canebière, with the message *'a little something to ease the long voyage – Bausch.'*

The two guards appeared confused. They muttered between themselves and for a split second, Eva thought they would be caught. After a few moments, one of the guards jerked his thumb.

"Yes, yes, go – you go now – be quick."

Both women got out and as the men watched Eva pull down her skirt, Olga shot them both with a silencer.

Brandt got out. His limbs ached with having been huddled up in a cramped position, lying on the car's floor, covered with a blanket. Glancing around to see if they had been noticed, he dragged the men over to the side and pushed them down between the ship and the quay.

"Eva, stay in the car. Stay low. If I'm not back in twenty minutes, drive off."

"Be careful."

He kissed her.

Brandt walked quickly, disguised in his heavy fatigues and woollen hat pulled low. He swung the canvas kit bag onto his shoulder, masking his face and he quickly found the engine room through the warren of corridors. He knew all of Jongbloed's hiding places and checked them all. The engine room was deserted. Working quickly, he placed the plastic explosives and their charges at the critical sections of the diesel engines. He packed as much as he could on the drive shafts and bearings. He swaddled them in heavy grease. It had been his home for nearly a month and he felt a moment of sadness at what he was doing. He primed the timers and left the engine room, the whole operation took five minutes. Below decks, the ship was deserted, occasional clangs and footfalls rang out overhead indicating some crew were aboard.

He glanced quickly into Jongbloed's quarters. Both bunks were stripped down and any sign of habituation removed. Though not a religious man, Brandt muttered a simple prayer for the Afrikaan. He hoped he survived the journey and was hiding out somewhere in Marseilles, enjoying a cognac. He smiled at that thought.

It was dark when he left the ship and it took a few moments for his eyes to adjust to the gloom. The Bugatti had moved away. He found it parked close to a stack of packing crates. He gave a low whistle. The car's headlights flashed once. His heart raced at seeing Eva again, then reality set in; they could be dead in a heartbeat if they didn't get off the quay. The car was already running as he jumped in the passenger side.

In the Bugatti's wing mirrors, they saw a thick cable of smoke rise from the freighter's aft section. Muted pops and bangs drifted in through the car windows as Eva expertly shifted gears and hurtled Bausch's Bugatti through the city streets.

***

Chainbridge had laid out the contents of Bausch's attaché case on the small table in the safe house in Marseilles. It offered little. Various sealed documents signed by Bormann; maps, schedules, contact names for the party at the hotel. Chainbridge went through the stack of papers page by page. When he had finished, he removed the lamp shade on the table and held each paper in front of the naked bulb. On a piece of headed stationery carrying Foucault's crest, something caught his eye.

"Erik."

Kant looked up from his post watching the street through the closed drapes. On the table he had stacked his magazines and cigarettes. One was permanently lit in the ashtray. He walked over and without breaking a beat, Hauptman rose and took his place at the window.

"Herr Chainbridge?"

"Numbers and co-ordinates, they're your speciality aren't they? The watermark – what are those under it?" Kant leaned in squinting, the watermark was German, and just below it was a series of numbers.

"Hauptman."

Bader took point. Without looking down, he pulled a match from Kant's matchbook, prised off the head and jammed the matchstick into the corner of his mouth. He watched the street though his rifle's telescopic sight.

The three men studied the page. After a moment Hauptman said:

"Looks like the numbers of a train timetable, without the column lines."

Chainbridge exhaled slowly.

"Bloody hell. A departure time or an arrival time?"

Once Michelet's name had been mentioned by Eva in Foucault's private box at the races, a file had been opened on him by Int. 7. Michelet had a private train, and a train could ship anything, anywhere once over the border into Germany.

They have a back-up plan, once Eva was discovered, thought Chainbridge.

The gun was being shipped by train across the Reich.

Damn.

Kramer who had been hiding in a doorway across the street, threw a small pebble at the window.

Chainbridge turned the lamp off.

"It's Brandt, Olga and Eva," said Kant peeping through the drapes.

"I'll contact Bracken."

He went through the pages again, to see if anything connected. He went back to the case, it was beautifully stitched and its very touch indicated superior craftsmanship. He ran his fingers around the edges, looking for a secret compartment. He fished in his pockets and found his pen-knife. Working it into the stitching he opened the seams and found what he was looking for; a secret compartment. Inside was a strip of silk ribbon onto which were written a radio band width, a date, time and grid co-ordinates.

Eva, Brandt and Olga sat around the table. For the first time since October 1941 his team were gathered in the sa me spot. Chainbridge handed around the ribbon.

"I know the band width," murmured Bader, a lean man, with dark eyes and a quiet solidity about him. "It's SS Crimea."

"Same with the co-ordinates; 44° 56' 53" N, 34° 6' 15". I'm pretty sure at a glance, they're inside Russia," said Brandt.

"Urus Martan," said Chainbridge.

"Where?" said Brandt.

"Near my country," said Olga. The only person who had heard her speak was Kant. Her German, though stilted, had a sonorous quality, "The mountains of Chechnya."

"A mountain range. They're excavating the side of a huge mountain," said Chainbridge.

Brandt looked up at Chainbridge,

"Big enough to house a super-gun?"

"It would appear so," replied Chainbridge.

"We've blown up the Chateau and have discovered the gas centrifuge there. And hopefully, crippled the freighter," said Brandt.

"But not Foucault's yacht and Guy Michelet owns a private train," said Chainbridge

He donned his coat and hat.

"We still have work to do, gentlemen."

He had to get word to the Americans.

TWENTY-TWO
Norfolk shipyard, U.S.A.

McElhone watched the transfer of President Franklin D Roosevelt from his yacht *Potomac* to the USS Iowa. At moments like this, the president's discomfiture at being hoisted in a wheelchair, made everyone look away briefly. Within minutes, the President was welcomed aboard by Iowa's captain, McCrea. The ship's dog, Vicky, caught Roosevelt's eye and the wheelchair's height had the sudden advantage of allowing the President reach the dog's muzzle. Vicky's bushy tail wagged vigorously as the President rubbed her gently around the ears. She leaned against the chair's wheel as the Joint Chiefs of Staff, their entourage and Roosevelt's security team boarded.

McElhone was the last to board. He looked out over the sea as the battleship got underway.

Being a superstitious man, Roosevelt insisted the flotilla set sail after midnight.

"The President will see you now," said an armed marine.

McElhone was led to the Iowa's ready room. Roosevelt sat behind a huge mahogany desk. His head, in profile appeared leonine. Standing beside him was William J. Donovan, head of the OSS.

"Mr. President, Mr. Donovan."

"Thank you, agent McElhone, for arriving at such short notice. I've appraised President Roosevelt and he requested we meet immediately."

McElhone was in his mid-forties. He had been a serving detective in the New York police department, but had been unceremoniously removed from his post by Donovan's rival, J. Edgar Hoover. Donovan had thrown him a lifeline with the OSS.

The tall New Yorker opened the case cuffed to his wrist and presented the documents. In the stark ships lighting, Roosevelt looked drawn, ill, his inner light fading with every sigh and movement.

Bracken's Int. 7 offices had successfully transmitted a photographic image of long tubes beside the hull of a ship. Though grainy and incomplete in places, the transmission contained enough detail to be added to the intelligence files.

"Mr Churchill has the same intelligence on his ship?"

The voice McElhone had heard nearly every day on the radio over the past ten years, had a reedy quality to it. It made him uncomfortable.

"He does, Mr. President."

Roosevelt and Donovan pored over the papers.

"Edward Patrick McElhone," said Roosevelt, "is that a New York accent?"

"It is, Mr. President, I'm from Clinton and Midtown West."

"Hell's Kitchen," smiled Roosevelt. "Mr Donovan here is a New Yorker too. Tough people."

He put his glasses down.

"How credible is this threat, agent McElhone? If Mr. Donovan thinks I need to see this, then I like to meet the messenger before I go back to the joint chiefs."

McElhone thought for a moment.

"The team that have sent this were the same ones who disrupted the Zinnman rocket, and Mr. Curran, who alerted us to this threat, is travelling with Prime Minister Churchill. If they say Hitler has a super-gun capable of reaching a target of in excess of a thousand miles, then we should take it seriously."

Roosevelt sat back and twisted a cigarette into its tortoise shell holder. Lighting it, he puckered it into the corner of his mouth and tilted it upward at a jaunty angle.

"Do we know the target?" he asked.

"Possibly Moscow, but Tehran is feasible, Mr. President."

"Damn. Is it possible, Bill? Distance, wind-speed, weather factors?"

Donovan took his time, slowly perusing the documents.

"Hitler's rolling the dice on super weapons, Mr. President. SOE and their colleagues in Int. 7 have confirmed that to be the case. You say, Mr. McElhone, that an advanced targeting system has been developed for this gun?"

"We think so, but cannot confirm, Director, Mr. President."

McElhone remembered Donovan's advice on appraising the president – be honest. He felt the deck below his feet tilt as the Iowa carved her way into the Atlantic Ocean.

Roosevelt looked up.

"Okay, I'll contact Chairman Stalin and alert him; it's in his backyard, so he has to clean it up. We'll offer any and all assistance. Thank you Mr. McElhone, I'll ask you to leave now, but just so you know, you're coming to Tehran."

"Thank you, Mr President, Mr. Donovan."

McElhone wanted to shake the leonine president's hand, but saluted instead.

The armed marine escorted him to his berth below decks. He climbed into his bunk and felt the ship lurch wildly, he stared up at the metal bulkhead; Tehran.

"What do think, Bill?" Roosevelt asked.

"I think Europe's a side-show, Mr. President. I agree, let Stalin sort this one out. Besides, the trail went cold in France, those barrels, tubes, whatever they are could be anywhere by now."

"Let's get to Cairo first, Bill, then worry about Tehran when it comes."

Roosevelt looked at the grainy photograph and intelligence memos one more time.

"You know, Bill, I used to own this boat; the Larooco. She was a crock – engines never worked, we always seemed to wind up beached on sand banks – I loved her. Anyway, Bill, we all went shark fishing one day, saw this fin, huge fish, one mean bad fish, he always kept one step ahead of us, never took the bait. Always wondered about him. That's where we're headed, Bill; we're going swimming with a big Russian shark in Tehran."

"And have to deal with another one in Berlin."

"Let them tear each other apart, Bill, that's what I say, pick up the pieces afterwards."

"Mr President. The joint chiefs?"

"They've enough on their plate without this. Say nothing for now."

Roosevelt leaned back in his wheelchair.

"Let the American Legation, Tehran, start checking things out; Mike Reilly there, should be appraised."

He stared at the grainy image of the Bakelite tubes transmitted in minutes across thousands of miles,

"Anyway, Bill, these tubes are probably gold-plated plumbing for the Eagle's nest's crapper."

The Iowa and her escorts ploughed into the Atlantic Ocean. It was Saturday morning.

TWENTY-THREE

Gare St. Charles train station, Marseilles

Foucault was concerned. Neither Michelet nor Bausch had been in contact. He found it very vexing. He debated opening one of Dr. Morell's pick-me-ups but decided against it.

"They're late," said Hoeberichts. The city heat didn't seem to improve his complexion any. Ram-rod straight in his seat, he opened an old fashioned pocket watch.

"There was a fire," said Foucault.

"A fire?" replied Hoeberichts. He turned the winder with slow deliberation.

"We can't reach them and we can't investigate, there's Vichy gendarmes, though. The prefect of Police has told me his best men are there," said Foucault.

"That doesn't instil much confidence," replied Hoeberichts.

"Captain Eklund informed me his engine room was sabotaged."

"Liquidate him," said Hoeberichts

"Already done," said Foucault.

"The chief engineer?"

"They found him hiding in a forward hold. He's now dead."

"Unfortunate. Interrogated?"

"Died as a result of his questioning. Nothing useful I'm afraid," replied Foucault.

Hoeberichts stared at Foucault.

"I don't believe in coincidences, and there are too many at the moment, Herr Foucault."

"Lord will suffice. We're two days behind schedule, acceptable in my opinion," replied Foucault.

Hoeberichts' heterochromatic stare burned deep.

"Unacceptable to me. The U-235?"

"Transferred to *Serenity*. Michelet managed sixteen kilos of useable uranium."

"That's enough," said Hoeberichts.

He replaced the watch and poured some vodka into his coffee. His flask was gold with rich inlays of precious jewels. He slipped it back into his three quarter length leather coat.

After a nervous few moments when their papers were examined by grim-faced Gestapo and Vichy French Police, Eva and Olga found a table at a bustling café in the station. They were dressed as nuns from the order Religieuses du Sacre Coeur de Jesus. A coded message from the Jesuits had reached Chainbridge. Foucault and Michelet had ensured the departure of Michelet's armoured train be allowed to travel through all points.

Around the station were posters of Paris, Edith Piaf and Jane Sourza along with the Vichy flag and portraits of Hitler. A poster reading 'Revue Negre, au Music-hall, Champs Elysees, Paris' with a picture of Josephine Baker dancing with a jazz trio had been defaced with the German scrawl 'nigger, kike, jungle music'.

The poster must have been well pasted onto the wall as very little of it had been torn off. It made Eva smile.

The café was bustling with lounging German officers who were saluted by passing soldiers, plain clothes police and Gestapo as they read the morning newspapers.

Eva paid for the coffees, the waiter treated it like a benediction. They spied Foucault, surrounded by Waffen SS soldiers, Wiking Korps. Feral dogs primed for the smallest gesture from their master.

Eva then noticed young people around the station wearing the heavy lumber jackets that Mireille's team wore, the girls in dressed in fake furs and short skirts. The woman sitting beside her, watching them and assuming the order's habit was some cloth of confidentiality, whispered:

"Zazous, we defy the Nazi's with our wonderful fashion style!'

Eva smiled. Beneath her habit, strapped to her thigh, was a pouch containing a fast-acting sedative.

Outside in a waiting delivery van was Mireille and one of her team.

Olga nudged Eva slightly.

Foucault was on the move.

"Ready?" whispered Eva.

Olga nodded.

"I need to stretch my legs," said Foucault. He spotted two pretty nuns sitting across from him. "I fancy a spot of corruption with a Vot'ress…"

"Ten minutes, Charles," said Hoeberichts, his skeletal skull had finally decided to perspire.

"Won't be a jiffy, old boy."

He eased his way past his security detail. Hoebericht's motioned for one of the troopers to follow.

"Merde," whispered Eva.

Foucault strode across the station with an assured gait, his very gravitas making people side-step him without him breaking his stride.

His bodyguard strutted a few feet behind. His rifle slung over his shoulder.

Suddenly a Zazou girl dashed up to him and put her arms around him, caught off guard, his helmet clattered onto the floor.

Foucault pulled a chair up to Eva and Olga. Raised his arm into the air and clicked his fingers for service.

Eva thrust the syringe into his thigh.

His grin slipped for a second as he recognised her. Then he slumped over the table.

The trooper threw the girl aside, punching her full force in the face. The girl screamed. It echoed around the station.

Eva heaved Foucault up.

"You!" he slurred.

People stopped to look at the commotion. The Zazou was screeching, punching the SS trooper and cursing him. Unslinging his rifle, he drove the butt of it into her face. She fell like a tree.

He heard a whistling sound, then felt a blow to his solar plexus. His hand reached up to the knife sticking out of it.

Olga Mirinova never missed.

Screams, shouts and police whistles rang out and a cluster of men and women stood over the fallen trooper. The Zazous had disappeared in the melee, ushered out by French resistance.

"Stay!" Barked Hoeberichts pointing to the nuns escorting Foucault toward the entrance. His voice was lost in the commotion.

He took a rifle from one of his troopers; a reconditioned Gewehr 98.

Eva and Olga guided Foucault through the throng with an air of concern. Eva had told several passers-by in the pandemonium that Foucault had fainted.

Over the shouts and screams, they didn't hear the first shot. The second one lifted Olga off her feet and slammed her across the floor.

Eva couldn't hold Foucault as he spilled with her onto the Chechen.

Hoeberichts smiled thinly as he lowered the rifle.

"Bring them to me."

The remaining troopers began to force their way through the crowd.

Eva hoisted Foucault up. Olga wasn't moving. The tiles around her were covered in blood.

Mireille appeared near the entrance, she dashed to them.

"Leave her. She's dead."

"I can't. We just can't leave her."

"Go."

Eva dragged Foucault out through the entrance and down the flights of steps. From within the station the crackle of machine gun fire rang out. It was followed by the pops of rifles and the screams of terrified commuters.

The delivery van was waiting. Eva hurled Foucualt into the back, assisted by the young man she had met in the forest.

She checked the breech of Michelet's gun.

"No. You can't," hissed the boy.

Whistles and sirens filled the streets. A truckload of soldiers pulled up and began cordoning off the area.

"We have to go. Allez."

With tears in her eyes, Eva climbed into the vehicle. It slowly accelerated so as not to draw attention. Once out of the city limits, the young man accelerated to the rendezvous.

***

Olga was with her grandfather again, they were walking in her village, his hand warm and calloused, hers, small. She was a child again.

"Wait," she said.

He stopped.

"Not yet," she whispered.

Her eyes fluttered open. She was cold. Her brain instructed her limbs to move, but there was no response.

She thought of Kant. He had rescued her from a lynch mob on the Eastern front two years earlier. They had loved and shared many close shaves, but today she was going to die. She hated leaving him behind to fend for himself; the big lumbering fool.

The faces looking over her had their teeth bared like animals; she didn't have the strength to fend the first blows of the rifle butts.

She took her grandfather's hand. He used to always whistle three bars of a song when he was happy. Olga whispered,

"Now."

TWENTY-FOUR
Simferopol, Crimea

The first of the early snow flurries danced around the boots of SS-Obergruppenführer Hoeberichts. He stamped his feet to increase the circulation, his heavy leather greatcoat fastened against the cold.

In the harbour, the Englishman's yacht, *Serenity* was at anchor. They had made good time. She had her cargo of pharmaceuticals for his troops offloaded along with enough U-235 for two firings. His troops had off loaded the medicine, the local population, the radioactive materials. She was flanked by two U-boats further out in the harbour. They glinted like knives in the water. The area they were standing in was a wasteland cleared of any inhabitants and woodland. The Bakelite tubes, shipped on Hoebericht's armoured train had been opened by local work gangs and the barrels of *'Thor's Hammer'* lay on the ground.

It was unfortunate that Foucault had gone missing in the melee at the train station. The nun with the knife had died on the stations floor before he could get to her.

Coincidences. There was no such thing.

His adjutant, Schelling, looked out over the bay through high powered binoculars.

"Here they come, sir.

Hoeberichts scanned the horizon through his binoculars and smiled at the sight. Two airships, the size of horizontal skyscrapers hummed over the ocean on huge engines. They were requisitioned soviet ships, each three hundred and forty feet long, silver and with the red white and black livery of the swastika.

"And on time, too, Schelling."

The two mammoth dirigibles glided toward land with immense grace and power. Twenty minutes passed until they hovered overhead and chains and hooks fell from them to the ground. The men of Hoeberichts' Wiking division secured the barrels with the chains and steel cradles, stripped to the waist and sweating from the exertion.

"The crews think the loads will be ready by late afternoon, sir."

Hoeberichts grunted.

"Are the barrels intact?"

"Not a scratch, sir, the waterproof materials in the inner sections had held."

"Superb. Local Partisan groups?"

"Eliminated, sir."

"The work gang?"

"Dispatched to the concentration camp, sir."

Hoeberichts was a man who liked firm conclusions to any operation and disliked loose ends. He had overseen the construction of the gun site with cold and merciless perfection. His troops and engineers had excelled and he had made honourable mentions in dispatches. They had the breech installed ahead of schedule and the targeting computer had been run through its paces. The Breech was truly enormous; he had seen in rolled in from Czechoslovakia. It rolled on long re-enforced rails back into the depths of the mountain. The mountain itself would have to absorb the thousands of ton of recoil of 'Thor's Hammer' as the shell was launched.

With a mighty roar, the two airships rose into the late afternoon light, their silver skins blending with the pulses of snow around them.

"Urus Martan, Schelling," said Hoeberichts as he pulled the fur lined collar of his coat around his neck and pressed his peaked cap lower onto his shaven head.

"Urus Martan, SS-Obergruppenführer," replied Schelling. He gave a shrill whistle and his men dressed quickly in the cooling air.

Once in their uniform they stood to attention and raised their right arm to SS-Obergruppenführer Hoeberichts.

"Let Churchill, Roosevelt and that Georgian pig, Stalin get a taste of *Thor's Hammer*. To victory!"

"Heil Hitler!" bellowed his men.

"Heil Hitler," replied Hoeberichts. They filed aboard the two waiting troop transport aircraft and took off, accelerating past the airships and banking upward into the soviet skies.

Hoeberichts watched the airships pass below. The Heinkel's shadow flowed across the skin of the behemoths. His forward command had sent coded communiqués to Hitler's Rastenburg HQ, indicating the safe arrival of the gun components.

Then the consecration of the shells would begin.

"I flew on the Hindenburg in 1936," said Hoeberichts. "I was a champagne salesman – just like Ribbentropp, before he added the *'Von'*. Have you ever been to New York?"

Schelling stared out at the clouds.

"No, sir, I haven't."

"Amazing city. The Empire State Building is a thing of beauty. Soon, Schelling, we will add it to our Reich. Think of it, Schelling, we could be posted to New York, Washington DC, Paris even a neutral London in the next few years. Everything and anything is possible now, thanks to our glorious Führer."

He sat back and opened his sealed orders.

The location of the conference had been revealed – Tehran, day and date.

"Tell the crews at Urus Martan we have the target."

Schelling undid his seat belt and inched his way down the aircraft. He handed the radio operator the message. The operator began transmitting Hoeberichts' orders.

He reviewed intelligence reports for Tehran, topography, grid co-ordinates and long-range weather forecasts. The 'hollow point' where the shell would detonate, would turn ten miles of Tehran city into ash.

The second shell would be for Moscow.

He opened his second set of sealed orders, folded parchments with the blood-red wax stamped with the seal of the Ahnenerbe.

Within the sere pages, astrological charts and detailed lines of influence were meticulously drawn. The consecration would have to take place in the centre of a sonnenrad, and the nearest one was aboard *Serenity*. But it wasn't time. The planets and celestial bodies were not aligned.

Yet.

Through the cockpit, the clouds parted and the mountain of Urus Martan appeared. The transport began its descent, following the fighter escort that had scrambled to meet it.

Looking out, Hoeberichts could make out the deep gorge in the mountainside, camouflaged with hundreds of yards of green netting. Also concealed were banks of anti-aircraft gun emplacements and 88mm heavy guns.

The two H-11s landed and as he strode to his command tent, Hoeberichts could hear the distant drone of the airships engines. He paused to marvel at the vast vessels as they glided toward the mountains.

"How long, Schelling?"

"Should be here within the hour, sir. Luftwaffe's baby now."

With a deafening roar, ten Focke-Wulf FW 190's took off and rose from the site's airbase like a murder of crows to escort the incoming airships. Within minutes they were alongside the dirigibles, dwarfed by them. Once the squadron were within range, the ground based anti-aircraft guns swung into operation.

"Any Russian who fancies his chances now, will be turned to mincemeat," grinned Schelling.

"It was a Russian who let the location of the conference slip, Schelling, they must want to be rid of Stalin as much as we do."

"Let's oblige them, sir."

"Lets."

TWENTY-FIVE
Woburn, England

Peter de Witte inhaled deeply, the country air filled his lungs and the early morning dew seeped into his bones. He smoked quietly, shrugging himself deeper into his greatcoat. The distant squawk of crows broke the silence. The stately home he was standing outside of was prison to Rudolf Hess.

Martha touched his shoulder.

"Here they come."

She stepped inside the building. They had driven down in the early hours, Martha de Witte offering to drive rather than an M.T.C. driver. Although separated from her husband for nearly five years, she sensed the sands of time beginning to flow much faster between them. Normally a stubborn, proud, independent man, de Witte had acquiesced without a murmur –that alone, worried Martha.

De Witte could hear the vehicles approach, a car and the deeper grind of a van or truck. The staff car pulled up and de Witte recognised M.T.C. driver Knox's brisk footfall, the faint waft of her perfume as she opened the back door of the car. He heard SOE director Douglas Gageby wheeze as he alighted.

"Good morning, Peter, thank you for arriving at such short notice. Eva successfully extracted him in one piece. We had to scramble a Halifax bomber from Southern command; all very hairy by all accounts with the Luftwaffe. Ready?"

De Witte detected a limp in Gageby's stride, perhaps suggesting an underlying health issue.

"Ready. Chainbridge?"

"They've done their best; disabled the centrifuge and the freighter." Gageby's voice carried an undertone of deceit, thought de Witte.

"Have they recovered the material?"

"No. But this gentleman arriving, should enlighten us." Gageby's tone had hardened.

"Let's hope so."

From the back of the second vehicle, a battered furniture delivery van, Charles Foucault stepped down. He was unsteady on his feet and looked disorientated. He resembled a French nobleman on his way to the guillotine; haughty and indifferent. On either side of him were plain clothed, armed agents who assisted the hand-cuffed nobleman.

"Ah, Director Gageby, good morning." Foucault's voice cracked on the third syllable. He was terrified.

"Good morning, Charles," said Gageby.

"Is that a Sobranie cigarette, old boy?" Foucault called over to de Witte. De Witte opened his cigarette case and held it out.

"Dank je," said Foucault as he took one. De Witte opened his lighter and lit the cigarette. He had practiced this action to the point of perfection.

"A real pleasure to meet you, Peter de Witte."

De Witte remained silent as Foucault was ushered into the building. He extinguished his cigarette with his shoe.

The room was whitewashed with a concrete floor, sparsely furnished with a crudely made table and three chairs. Gageby and de Witte sat side-by-side facing Foucault. The room felt cold and damp. It was lit by a single overhead light bulb. Beneath the table, a microphone was fitted. Listening devices were embedded in the walls. In the adjoining room sat a recording engineer. A wire-tape machine was running, picking up every sound in the room.

"Shall we begin?" asked Gageby.

The door opened and an armed marine handed Gageby a thick manila folder.

"I think you may have over-stepped the mark, Gageby, old boy."

De Witte detected a tremor of fear beneath the cool, cadenced vowels. From the folder, Gageby produced Brandt's photograph of *the Aurora* in dry dock.

"Your friend, Lord Alfred Bevansdale's vessel, *the Aurora* in Buenos Aires a few weeks ago. Your company chartered it and filled it with a lot of material that isn't pharmaceuticals for the equine market. What's encased in the Bakelite around the hull?" said Gageby.

"I have no idea."

"Bevansdale is a known appeaser and friend of Goering. He has used his vessels to ship Spanish bullion during the Civil War."

"If you say so, I only met him on a couple of pheasant shoots. Is this the reason why I'm here?"

He was finding his feet, thought de Witte; he's starting to speak to Gageby as if he were the hired help.

"Manifest indicates 'oil pipeline equipment'."

Gageby was beginning to defer to him; the Nobleman knew it.

Foucault stared straight ahead.

After a beat, Gageby continued.

"They were observed being loaded, but when the vessel was searched, weren't on board."

Gageby produced another photograph, this one showed Foucault, Bausch and Hannah in the Teatro Colón Opera House talking to several men in evening wear.

"These gentlemen represent the Nationalsozialistsche Deutsche Arbeiterpartel, an organisation of German's living abroad and based in Buenos Aires."

Foucault winced at Gageby's German pronunciation and looked at the photograph.

"Fellow opera lovers, exchanging pleasantries. Who took the photograph?"

He remembered Eva had left his arm for half an hour that night.

"One of these men was pictured with you at a pheasant shoot in 1941," said de Witte. "Janick Frederik Rohmer, he was attaché to the German embassy in Spain."

De Witte paused. Gageby found the photograph and slid it over to Foucault. It was a grainy image of Foucault, Rohmer and another man; bloody Lord Alfred Bevansdale, plump and gurning. They were in hunting tweeds, but unfortunately for Foucault, none of them were wearing hats. It was clearly him.

"I can't say I remember, it was a busy season and he didn't introduce himself to me at the opera."

"Rohmer now works for Johann Wehrli & Company of Zurich, who have Swiss bank accounts for German companies working in Argentina. They are deeply involved in financing metallurgy, arms and munitions companies. They also support a company named Z-Weber-CH, which has ties with your own pharmaceutical company, through the late Sherman Harris the third."

"I have various contracts with European and American organisations, that's no secret."

Foucault longed for one of Dr. Morrell's pick-me-up powders.

De Witte leaned forward; his voice was pitched low, in a sincere manner, like a confessor.

"The Swiss banks are being difficult with our requests, so we took a different route and spoke to the Banco Aleman Transatlantico, where they confirmed after enormous pressure from our allies in

Washington, that you have assisted in transferring some of Martin Bormann's cash assets; several million, it seems."

"Again, I see no wrong-doing," said Foucault. The Dutchman had managed to wrong foot him, thought Gageby; he noticed Foucault's disdainful look.

Gageby cleared his throat.

"We have several options at our disposal here Foucault, you will certainly remain either at his majesty's leisure at the Tower of London. We can pump you full of drugs until you tell us everything…" From inside his jacket pocket, he produced a sheet of paper. "And there's this – an authorisation to hand you over to the Russian authorities. It's signed by Eden. We can have you inside Russia's borders within twenty-four hours. The Lubyanka, I believe, have somewhat more brutal methods at their disposal."

Foucault swallowed dryly.

"May I have a glass of water please?"

The room felt suddenly warm and cloying.

Gageby rose and opened the door, whispering to the guard.

"I have absolutely no idea what all this is about gentlemen." Foucault, aloof and composed again, raised his handcuffs. "Hardly the way to treat one, now is it?"

De Witte allowed a moment. He removed his jacket, draped it over the back of his chair, removed his cigarette case and opened it in the middle of the table. All three took one and lit up, Foucault sipped slowly from a chipped china cup.

"The Abwehr have a poste restante box in Dublin, PO Box 463. This is your handwriting, is it not?"

Gageby, with a delicate movement, produced an opened envelope with a swirling cursive style of writing on the front of it. Inside was a note *'NDA, shipping via RMS, 26 x Blite components + U235. Michelet enjoying the med.'*

Gageby then produced an Admiralty report drafted and signed by Foucault.

"The handwriting, as you can see, matches."

De Witte afforded himself a slight smile. Even though they had been apart, Martha had managed to set up a small allied network to monitor the Abwehr in neutral Ireland.

"U235 threw all of us," said de Witte quietly. "We thought it was a German submarine, but our contacts in Buenos Aries witnessed heavy lead containers being loaded alongside the Bakelite tubes. The sort of containers that would be needed to store and transport fissile materials safely. Why did you purchase these minerals and several tons of high tensile Bakelite?"

"My companies are commercial shipping, gentlemen. If this were the American Civil War, we'd be blockade running the Yankees. It's completely legitimate, it depends on your politics or point of view. Just because there's a war on, doesn't mean industry should stop."

He twisted and turned his Wat Tyler ring as he spoke.

"How do you know Guy Michelet?" asked Gageby.

Foucault leaned back and exhaled slowly.

"I have only one thing to say to you both; these days, this great nation of ours is more likely to see Russian T-34 tanks in the streets of London rather than German panzers or paratroopers. I don't want to witness that, gentlemen, or see our glorious empire sold off by the pound."

In a sudden movement, Charles Foucault brought his hand-cuffed arms up and before de Witte and Gageby could react, bit down on the thick winder of his Rolex watch.

He was dead before either man could get around the table to him.

"Bugger," murmured Gageby.

"I thought he had been searched for cyanide and stripped of any possible capsules, director."

"So did I."

"What about this Lord Bevansdale?" asked de Witte.

"He's moved everything out of the country to Portugal."

De Witte let his cigarette burn down slowly, the evidence was tenuous at best to take to Churchill, M15 and MI6.

But enough for a man to take his own life.

"We had better strip him and tear his businesses and properties apart. See if he can offer us any more clues. Thank you for your department's assistance, Director Gageby. I'll notify Bracken."

Two sentries entered and helped Gageby lift Foucualt.

"Director Gageby."

"Yes, de Witte?"

"Foucault knew our identities, *exactly* our identities."

"I know."

TWENTY-SIX
Gale Morghe Airport, Tehran

Colonel Marko Kravchenko had left the Soviet Union twice before. Once he had spent a week in Helsinki while the Politburo pondered his fate. During that time, he had been approached by a scholarly-type and his blind side-kick to join British Intelligence. At each prompt Kravchenko had responded with his name, rank and serial number. The second time in Istanbul, chasing down stolen Faberge eggs; he touched the burns on the side of his face gingerly at the memory. In just over three years, he had lost everything; wife, child and home. Now he was a Colonel and at every stage of this war had come out alive, when all he wanted was death.

He watched the American plane begin its final approach. The Soviet airbase was framed by the distant snow-capped mountains that shimmered in the heat. Rain clouds were gathering about the peaks.

"Three thousand Red Army in the city and we find the local police force is being run by the Americans," intoned Commissar Yvetchenko beside him.

Like Kravchenko, he was perspiring; it was an unseasonably mild October day.

"Are we not all allies, Russian, Iranian, British and American, Comrade Commissar?" Asked Kravchenko. His NKVD uniform chafed against his slowly healing skin.

"For now, Comrade Colonel."

Kravchenko had overseen the installation of the bugging devices in the Soviet Embassy. Their superior, Lavrentiy Beria, skulking around in the shadows of the embassy was an unseen, but an ominous presence.

Kravchenko watched the NKVD head of transportation, Comrade Arkadiev, step forward to the taxiing aircraft.

Mike Reilly, head of White House Security, strode confidently from the aircraft and shook his counterpart's hands briskly. He was a burly man, flanked by his detail, dressed in sharp, dark suits. The American suits and raincoats were expensively cut for the weather and their shoulder holsters, the Russian NKVD uniforms were not.

McElhone followed Reilly to a command post in the airport. It was an immense field tent that allowed what little breeze there was, flow in. They were met with smart salutes and freezing cold vodka.

The Americans were ushered to a table set for lunch – deep shelled oysters sat on beds of crushed ice. Loaves of fresh bread stood in line amid crystal glasses and pitchers of water. Kravchenko thought of the unremitting poverty of they passed in Tehran city as they drove to the airbase.

More vodka, more toasts: *To Roosevelt*, to *Comrade Stalin*, to *the end of Hitler*.

After the oysters, consommé accompanied by olives, celery and cucumber salad. More vodka. The meal was consumed in awkward silence.

"General Arkadiev, my boss, President Roosevelt, flies in. Period," reilly's voice was quiet, but insistent.

Yvetchenko translated, Arkadiev, sat granite-faced.

McElhone studied the maps spread across the table as Reilly spoke.

"Railway is too dangerous. We'll fly him in low over the mountains direct from Cairo."

McElhone watched the Russians, all looked battle-hardened. One nearest Yvetchenko was tall, with recent facial burns that were still raw-looking; his eyes took in everything.

"We would be more than happy for President Roosevelt to stay as a guest at the Soviet embassy. It is well protected. It is, secure."

Yvetchenko's English wasn't heavily accented; his voice had a quiet assurance, thought McElhone. It was in sharp contrast to his pit-bull mien. He watched the men around the Russian. He wielded power, and they feared and loved him at the same time. He pointed to a map hanging from the command post's ceiling.

"A Soviet operation is underway in the Northern region," continued Yvetchenko.

"German paratroopers?" asked Reilly. The mood around the table shifted. It required more vodka.

"Merely a security sweep, nothing to worry about."

"We've heard different." Replied Reilly.

Being around Roosevelt every waking hour for twelve years, gave his voice the same flinty edge. He nodded to McElhone. McElhone produced an envelope from his jacket and placed it on the table. Kravchenko opened it. Inside was the grainy photograph of the Bakelite tubes. With it, a translation of the co-ordinates of Urus Martan and aerial reconnaissance photos.

"The Germans have a super gun. One capable of firing a warhead out of occupied Russia. British Intelligence has all the details there," said Reilly.

Yvetchenko remained impassive. He took the sheaves of intelligence.

"We will look into it, thank you."

He handed it to one of the waiters hovering nearby. He took it and left.

One of the American transport pilots stepped into the tent and whispered to Reilly. A distant drone filled the air outside.

"Gentlemen, if you would follow me please," said Reilly.

Outside in the shimmering heat, a silver pencil-shaped aircraft appeared, banking low over the mountains. As it drew nearer, the four sleek engines thundered on wings that seemed to go on forever.

"Naturally, President Roosevelt is happy to extend our resources to address this threat. It's a prototype; a high altitude bomber with a payload to deal with the problem."

Yvetchenko and the NKVD stood in silence as the aircraft, catching the sun's rays like Ezekiel's chariot, began to lower her undercarriages.

"Have you someone who can fly one of these things?" asked Reilly.

"Yes," said Yvetchenko, the pilot he had met at Kursk; Ivana Troyanovskii, the petite beauty who had flown him to the maw of hell; he thought of what this weapon could do to a city the size of Tehran.

"I do."

Across the desert, a convoy of American jeeps appeared.

"Thanks for the hospitality, Commissar Yvetchenko, General Arkadiev," said Reilly.

"Please consider The Russian Embassy," said Arkadiev.

"I'll advise you once we've checked out the rest of Tehran, General."

Amid the jeeps and armed marines, the US Ambassador's car pulled up.

"Good hunting," said Reilly.

Yvetchenko saluted briskly, then turned to Kravchenko.

"Ready to take the battle to the krauts, Comrade Colonel?"

TWENTY-SEVEN
France

She couldn't stop the bleeding. Hans Bader was dying. Mireille tried to staunch the flow from his chest, but it was constant. His shirt was soaked with it. The heavy towel she pressed against was drenched. With every swerve and pothole, the bleeding increased. Eva drove the delivery van flat out. Snatches of countryside went flashing by in the headlights.

"Not far now," she said.

In the rear mirror, she spied the distant headlights accelerating up the road; there was no way the van would outrun them.

Brandt was thinking the same thing.

"Pull over."

The attempt to de-rail Michelet's armoured train had failed. The sheer weight of the reinforced locomotive had rolled through the detonation. If there had been more plastic explosive, possibly; with what they had, pointless. The difference wasted on *Aurora*'s engine room. Then the machine guns had opened up from hidden slats along the side of the train, high velocity bullets hitting Bader square on and grazing Kramer. He sat in the back of the van with Bader's head resting listless on his lap.

Bader coughed up more blood. He was strong; it would take him some time to die.

Once they passed a hairpin bend. Eva brought the van to a halt.

Brandt jumped out.

"Kant."

Opening the van's door, they pulled out the remaining equipment. After this, they were down to pistols and whatever bullets were left. Eva turned the engine off and dimmed the lights.

Bader and Kant crouched at the bend.

They could see the approaching lights. They could hear the delivery van's engine ticking over.

As the black Gestapo Mercedes Benz turned the bend, both men fired their Panzerfausts. The car rode skyward scattering occupants, engine components and burning metal. It sailed over a stone wall, landing on its roof.

It burned intensely.

Brandt and Kant stood over each of the four men and shot them through the head.

It bought them time, but not much. They took the fallen men's service pistols and ran back to the van.

**

After the attempted derailment, Brandt had hot-wired a truck, with Bader critical, he had driven manically to the outskirts of Marseilles. At an abandoned farmhouse they had met Eva and the young resistance fighter; Jules.

Mireille arrived an hour later, still dressed in her habit.

"They killed Olga," she said.

"I thought she was only injured?" said Eva.

"They beat her with rifle butts. Beat her for a long time after she was dead." Mireille wiped her tears roughly with the back of her hand.

Kant had sobbed, his long face buried in his hands. Brandt went to him and held his close friend's wracking frame.

"I hope the man you snatched was worth it," said Mireille to Eva.

"I hope so too," said Eva.

The Halifax bomber had landed at the transmitted co-ordinates. Eva, Chainbridge and Jules had got Foucault aboard, but the Germans had showed up and it was simply the fact that the bomber's sturdy airframe had been able to absorb the gun-fire they got Foucault out of France. Chainbridge had bundled himself aboard and held out his hand to her. The aircraft had gunned the engines and her last image was Chainbridge's gloved hand still extended out the door, grasping and clutching out at the air.

Every step they took; the Germans were always one step behind. A nagging fear inched its way into Eva; they weren't going to make it out of France alive.

"Bader's close now," said Kramer.

It had been a bad day.

"If we can get to Lyon," said Mireille, "I can get us into Switzerland."

"Lyon it is, then," said Brandt.

Mireille turned to young Jules, Eva noticed that his ears stuck out; he reminded her of a pretty mouse.

"Go. Now."

Jules looked at her uncertainly.

"Go!" hissed Mireille. She returned to nursing Bader. Jules left, his black heavy lumber jacket blending with the night.

Brandt leaned over his old comrade, Bader.

"We'll get you patched up in no time. Hang in there."

He didn't let Bader see his face as he rose. Kramer put a cigarette in Bader's mouth, the ash burned weakly in the dim light.

In a darkened corner of the ruin, Brandt shared a cigarette with Eva, they held each other as if the world was ending.

He took her hand and they crept into another small room. It smelled like a pantry.

"Brandt."

He kissed her.

"Not today, Eva. We're not going to die today."

She wished she could believe him.

He pulled her close. They kissed, tongues seeking out lost days, weeks and memories. He pulled her closer and his fingers reached up into the folders of her skirt.

"Brandt." She whispered.

His fingers sought her wetness and her hidden moist pearl.

"We must be careful, I know." He murmured, "Not a sound."

Her perfume, the smell of her hair and sweat enraptured him. Their kisses turned to bites and deep low gasps as he thrust himself quickly into her.

He held her as long as he could before breaking free and spilling his seed onto the floor.

Eva pushed against the wall and ran the tips of her fingers across his swollen gland and tasted the bitter heat of his semen on her tongue.

A man was dying on the far side of the wall and for a moment in time, neither one of them cared

***

Brandt jumped into the passenger seat while Kant pounded up to the back door.

"How far?" whispered Brandt.

"Another hour," replied Eva.

"We'll radio Int. 7 when we get there. You ok to drive?"

Eva gunned the engine and the delivery van sped away from the carnage.

The Mercedes burned like a beacon.

***

Chainbridge stood at Meenagh's grave. A simple wooden cross read: *Meenagh Chainbridge, 1902-1943; B.Bombay*. He planned to get a proper headstone once the world was at peace again.

They had met in Bombay, at an embassy ball. She had agreed to a dance, ignoring the baleful glances and sotto asides. She loved to waltz, and her sari had brought colour to the dour and the rigid night fifteen years ago.

He took some comfort from the fact she had been killed instantly when the shelter had taken a direct hit.

He was shaking from the November mist that chilled around him. The past four years of absences, duty and war spilled from his eyes.

Peter de Witte touched his shoulder. The two old soldiers held each other.

"Ready?" asked Curran. He stood a few feet back, clad in his green tweeds.

"Ready," said Chainbridge.

They walked toward Bracken's waiting staff car.

"Nothing from Brandt, Eva?" asked Chainbridge.

"Nothing. They couldn't stop the train," said de Witte.

"The gun components on board?"

"Possibly," replied de Witte.

"It's up to the Russians then," said Chainbridge.

M.T.C. driver Knox stood and saluted smartly. She was out of uniform and dressed in a tunic and slacks. She wore a scarlet beret at a jaunty angle.

"Joining the organisation, Miss Knox?" asked Chainbridge.

She handed him an attaché case.

"Deborah, sir. The flying boat is ready for departure."

"Good luck, Henry," said de Witte. They shook hands. They both knew this would be the last time.

"Not travelling, Peter?"

"Not this time, my friend."

At least with Martha back by his side, he could begin moving past Eva.

Where the hell was Eva? he thought.

TWENTY-EIGHT
Urus Martan, Occupied Russia

Commander Dimitry Plutenko, of the 28th Light Infantry lowered his binoculars; he didn't need them to see the two huge airships.

Kravchenko stood beside him, shielding his eyes.

"CCCP-C's; originally Russian, captured by the Luftwaffe during the invasion."

"Very heavily defended, Comrade Commissar," said Plutenko.

A German fighter flew overhead.

Kravchenko moved as quietly as he could, scanning the vast site.

"Tell Stavka HQ we have found two airships and they are off-loading long tubes."

The radio operator cranked his transmitter and whispered into his head set. Over the ridge behind them, thirteen thousand men were waiting. Heavy T-34 tanks and trucks pulled racks of katyusha rockets and their crews were preparing to fire them.

"He's spotted us," said Plutenko.

The German fighter banked in a circle and flew low, his on-board cannons beginning to strafe the Red Army. The Luftwaffe base's klaxons began a murderous wailing and the sound of German aircraft being readied drifted across the site.

"Okay, Plutenko. Let them have it."

The katyusha rockets leapt from their launchers, raining screaming destruction onto the base. One rocket pierced the hull of the first airship. It ignited the hydrogen within. The stricken vessel immolated from bow to stern, lighting up the skyline with the inferno.

The first wave of Red Army to the minefields were the *Smertniki*; penal units. The minefields bloomed soil and body parts.

Kravchenko wanted to join in, to die and to finally shake the terrible burden of life.

"No, Comrade Colonel. Please remain here," said Plutenko.

He led the charge down the slope and with his men dodged through the cleared minefields and into the jaws of German machine guns. Through his binoculars, Kravchenko saw Plutenko had lost his helmet, a wild shock of blond hair sprouted from the Commander's crown. He threw grenades and crouched, spraying his targets with machine gun fire.

He had covered a lot of ground. He and his men had reached the barb-wire fence.

Kravchenko ordered mortar fire to land a hundred yards ahead of Plutenko.

The second airship released the chains containing the barrels. They fell like the hammers of the gods onto the scattering ground crews and SS troops.

Radios cracked around Kravchenko's command. The pops and cackle of machine-gun fire told them the Russians had engaged with the Wiking Korps.

A runner appeared, carrying an order from Stavka HQ.

"Send the order to fall back," said Kravchenko.

Radios were furiously cranked. Barked commands were met with shouts and cries from the Soviet forces below, and more often than not, just empty static.

They only had a few minutes.

***

Ivana Troyanovskii was dwarfed by the prototype bomber's cockpit controls. Smoothly she banked the plane, every component responding to her assured touch. She enjoyed the luxury of a pressurised cabin. Through the great glass cockpit, the world swept below her. The newer functions on the display had crude Russian descriptions in crayon pasted above them.

The navigator rechecked the co-ordinates, using a slide rule, map and stop-watch. The bombardier, a petite muscovite with blood-red lipstick, looked through the bombsite.

An immense explosion lit up the viewfinder – it had once been an airship. Another one was pulling away and ascending, fleeing to a higher altitude.

The muscovite held her breath.

And released the American bomb.

Serenity, had raised anchor in Simferopol harbour once Urus Martan had been attacked. It was purely a precautionary measure as the Russian air force was in the area. Satisfied his troops were maintaining the upper hand, Hoeberichts left the bridge and donned his silken vestments.

In Foucault's state room Hoeberichts lit the final candle on the sonnenrad. He was alone. Two Waffen SS troopers stood outside. In the centre of the circle, two tall copper-head artillery shells sat side-by-side. He smoothed each warhead casing with a stone made of Malachite. Beneath his feet he had inscribed a chart. Midheaven was neatly intersected with various lines; he had charted the weapon's birth and through careful calculation; plotted the perfect moment for the anointment.

The candle light flickered off them, up into the crystal chandelier and danced on Hoeberichts' Nepalese headdress.

He began his incantation. He poured the blood taken from the arm of Bormann's girl, Marianne, in Paris,

"I summon the fallen to guide the artillery shell to its target, straight and true."

Hoeberichts shook the incense burner in time to his chant.

The twelve candles standing proud on the points of the circle began to gutter and spit.

The maid's blood flowed along the shells casing, pooling in the nicks and burrs.

Standing before the second shell, Hoeberichts could almost sense the Aryan spirits of aeons ago flow and weave about him. The air became suddenly icy. As he poured the remaining blood over the second shell, he shook the burner with greater intensity, his chant becoming an invocation.

One-by-one in counter-clockwise sequence, a heartbeat apart, the candles began to extinguish.

As the last drop fell from the phial onto the weapon, the final candle went out.

"It is done," he murmured.

He heard the loudest thunder-clap ever. It resounded around the cabin. Louder than the one he had heard standing in the sun lounge of Hitler's Eagle's nest in September 1939.

The shockwave followed a few seconds later.

Serenity titled wildly, pitching Hoeberichts off his feet. The two huge shells keeled over with a deafening boom, colliding with several candles. They demolished one of the room's pillars. The ship kept on listing and Hoeberichts and several pieces of furniture slid down the polished floor.

Serenity reached her tipping point and time hung, suspended.

Hoeberichts landed on the far wall which had now become the floor. Books, chairs and a huge leather settee became missiles pounding and clattering around him. The portrait of Hitler glided down and landed at his feet. The Führer stared balefully out from the canvas. Behind it fell the mobile gun-rack. It spilled guns and cartridges everywhere. Hoeberichts clambered toward the water-tight door. The only light filtered in through the shattered portals.

Serenity lurched further. Two deafening peals told Hoeberichts, the copper-head shells had come to rest behind him.

Slowly, painfully, with deep groans around her keel and bulkheads, the yacht righted herself. Hoeberichts became airborne and landed in the middle of the sonnenrad.

He heard the rumble of the warheads spinning toward him.

He staggered to the door and prised it open.

Above decks, Hoeberichts stood and looked out at the harbour. The yacht's decks were littered with debris.

Most of Simferopol's buildings appeared intact. His staff car and armoured carrier though lay on their sides at the quayside. Several supply ships had taken the brunt. Two were ablaze, one was sinking.

The U-boats were gone.

"The Captain is dead, the first mate, missing," said Schelling. He had a handkerchief pressed against a gaping wound in his forehead. In his other hand was Hoeberichts' sable hat.

An explosion rumbled below decks.

"There go the kitchens," said Schelling.

Hoeberichts looked past the devastation to Urus Martan. It glowed orange on the horizon. The cloud cover above it had a hole punched through it. He placed the sable hat with its glistening deaths head crest onto his furrowed pate.

"Schelling, find someone who can tell me if this vessel is capable of getting underway?"

He was thankful the two shells he had consecrated below hadn't been primed.

TWENTY-NINE
Lyon

It had taken a day for Hans Bader to die. Brandt had prayed over him with Kramer, Kant and Hauptman. The hardest part was to come.

"Let me do it, sir," said Kramer. The oldest of the team, he had been in a concentration camp and had tended to his dying wife, Pilar, there.

His upper arm was covered in blood, both his and Bader's.

"No," said Brandt.

Bader had perfect teeth. They had to be removed. Taking a deep breath, using both ends of Carrington's heavy knife, he began removing them.

"Forgive me, old friend," he whispered. Nothing, not even dental records could lead the Gestapo back to them.

When he was finished, he started cutting off the tips of Bader's fingers. There wasn't enough petrol to burn his body.

Eva and Mireille stood guard, pistols primed. They were red-eyed and edgy from lack of sleep. A coded knock came to the safe house door.

Everyone held their breath.

Opening the door, a crack, Mireille smiled at the pretty mouse Jules. He was with two young men in the uniform heavy lumber jackets of the Zazous.

"Ready to go, boss?" he asked.

It was nearly nightfall.

"My friend died," said Brandt. "He must not be discovered."

"Leave it to me," replied Jules.

"Give him a Christian burial. He wouldn't want it, though."

Brandt looked back into the house. From the main sitting room, he could see Bader's legs sticking out on the floor.

In Brandt's tunic were Bader's teeth and finger tips.

They stepped out, glancing up and down the narrow street. Waiting for them was the delivery van. It had new livery on its sides and several bumps and dents had been crudely panel-beaten out. Bader's blood had dried into the vehicles boards. It was hurriedly covered by woven sacks.

Jules drove carefully, anticipating checkpoints. Brandt watched through a canvas drape that separated the driver from the back.

He didn't like it; he didn't like it one bit.

They arrived at the 4th arrondissement of La Croix, in the old city.

"You have very powerful friends," said Jules, as he let them out. They ducked out from the street and into a house. Jules opened the door that led to the subterranean passage.

"The train will wait for you at Bellegarde-sur-Valarine; but you haven't long. Here are your papers, identity cards and Swiss passports. Bon chance."

Mireille led the way through the traboule with a torch. Once their eyes adjusted they found smooth man-made walls that intersected at junctions. When they came out at the banks of the river, a barge was waiting for them.

Eva kissed Mireille tenderly.

"Join us."

The exotic resistance fighter held her close.

"My war is here. Be careful, ma cher. *Very* careful.."

Within moments, Mireille was underground.

The dour tiller man of the barge ushered them below with a jerk of a thumb. Warm coffee and bread waited for them. Thick blankets were stacked neatly on comfortable settles.

"Nobody speak," said Brandt.

The barge slipped its moorings and glided into the waterways.

Brandt went top-side to smoke. The putt-putt of the engine was soothing. He started dropping Bader's teeth and fingers into the oily water; a burnt offering to Lugis; bringer of light. As well as guiding them, Mireille had given them a history lesson.

"Our revels are now ended," he murmured.

Eva slipped her arms around him and kissed his greasy forehead.

"You smell, Brandt."

"You're no great shakes yourself, Eva. You should sleep."

They stared out at the riverbanks. Lyon was in darkness. Searchlights fanned the skyline and danced off the clouds.

"I'm sorry for Bader and Olga," she murmured.

"He was a good friend. Kant's a broken man."

He stared at her with a sudden intensity.

"I don't know what I'd do if I lost you, Eva."

"You'd survive, Brandt. We all do in the end."

She took the cigarette out of his mouth and kissed him tenderly. They huddled together on the barge and watched the river flow.

The first bullet struck the barge along the bow. Splinters of it popped up and spun on the breeze. They were passing under the low Passerelle Paul Couturier Bridge. The second burst tore up the roof they were sitting on. Brandt gave a grunt. Eva screamed.

The barge passed under the bridge and Eva called down.

"Machine gun!"

Kant appeared and scrambled up along the roof. Crouching over Brandt, he brought up his Haenel 41, shielding his fallen friend.

"Very low on ammo," he hissed.

Brandt gave a gasp.

"Shoulder, think it's passed through." Said Brandt.

Wincing, he felt through the sodden material. The entry point was small. His shoulder blade felt as if a burning poker had been jammed into it. He was losing a lot of blood.

The barge was coming out to the other side. The sullen tiller man without warning, jumped overboard.

"Not good." said Brandt.

"If they have grenades up there, we're finished," said Kant.

Without a tiller man, the barge began to drift.

Eva checked the breech on Michelet's pistol. She had five rounds in the clip, one in the chamber. Enough.

Kramer's head appeared at the back of the barge, he set a heavy machine gun up.

The barge cleared the other side of the bridge.

A heavy burst of fire from the bridge scattered them.

Brandt by instinct, rolled away, but slid off the roof and fell backwards into the water. The river's unforgiving water swept over him.

Eva fired up at the form holding the machine gun. The ears couldn't be mistaken; it was Jules.

Kant and Kramer caught him in a crossfire and Jules danced and whirled in his death throes. He fell backwards as Eva aimed between his pretty little mouse ears and fired four times in quick succession. Jules' head jerked and came apart.

"Brandt!" she yelled.

The waters were silent.

Kramer, scrambling across the roof, leapt down and took the tiller.

They peered over the murky waters.

Eva felt a finger of breeze and a whistling above her head. She ducked and looked at the canal bank. There was the unmistakable form of Hannah Wolfe. An imposing hour-glass figure was reloading a heavy rifle. A heavy transport truck skidded to a halt along the canal bank. SS troopers jumped out and trotted up to her.

She barked commands, jabbing her finger towards the barge. Three began assembling a heavy machine gun on a tripod.

"Christ – where did they come from?" hissed Kant.

Hannah squeezed off another shot. The bullet slammed into the side of the barge. A millimetre higher, it would have caught Eva in the groin.

Kramer swung the tiller, moving them slowly, too slowly, further into the river. Steadying herself Eva fired at Hannah. There was only the one round. Hannah spun, dropping the rifle, clutching her shoulder. Eva threw the pistol into the water.

She ducked down into the cabin.

A single Luger was all that was left. Mother of pearl handle with three rounds left.

For a second, she debated jumping overboard – they were sitting ducks.

Taking a deep breath and closing her eyes, she dashed back up into the fire-fight.

Kant picked off two of the SS tripod soldiers, forcing the third one to duck and then roll away.

The moon slipped behind a cloud, casting darkness across the river.

"Another bridge. About a minute." Roared Kramer. He was pushing and tugging the tiller, desperately trying to make the barge slalom through the water. He gave it pull, using all of his weight to rock the barge and make it a tricky target.

The water began to churn around them as the German patrol opened fire with machine guns. The cackle, pop and clack rang out across the water. The sides of the vessel began to splinter, Kant and Hauptmann spread themselves low on the roof, taking their time, selecting their targets. Two more Germans fell.

"Thirty seconds, we'll be under the bridge." Said Kramer.

The moon began to appear.

"Can't this thing go any faster for Christ's sake?" said Hauptmann.

A bullet tore through the roof beside him. 'Thirty seconds', in less than thirty seconds I am going to be dead, he thought.

More heavy fire rang out, this time it was along the canal bank it was Mireille and her Zazou comrades.

Grenade blasts scattered the Germans. Two French resistance fighters fell and the last thing Eva saw before the safety of the bridge, was Hannah jumping into the troop transport and driving off at high speed.

The shooting gradually stopped, but no German prisoners were taken.

"We have to turn around." Said Eva.

"We can't, reinforcements won't be far behind." said Kramer.

"We can't just leave him out there." Said Eva.

"Molenaar, we can't turn back." Said Kant. It was an intimidating whisper.

"You bastard, Kramer, that bastard, Jules." She said, "Brandt would go back for you!"

Kant placed a hand on Eva's arm. She pulled away.

"Brandt wouldn't go back. He'd leave. We have to get out of here."

Eva was wracked with sobs.

Somewhere across the city of Lyon, sirens began to wail.

"He's a good swimmer, like his father, Molenaar." Said Kant.

The barge was passing out from under the far side of the bridge.

"We can't just leave him out there." Whispered Eva.

"We go back. We die." Said Kant.

They all went below and began to pack up the remaining equipment.

Apart from pistols and knives, everything else was thrown overboard.

THIRTY

Tehran. The Russian embassy

McElhone and Chainbridge shook hands; they were dressed formally for the occasion and both felt out of place.

"So FDR's agreed to be Uncle Joe's guest? Every square inch will be bugged," said Chainbridge.

"The old man is well acquainted with them, Henry. I think he likes the idea. He's been mixing cocktails all evening for Churchill and Uncle Joe," smiled McElhone.

Roosevelt had flown in from Cairo, following Mike Reilly's route. It had taken eight hours for him to arrive.

There was a clatter from the reception area; someone had dropped a ceremonial sword. This was met with laughter, cheers and applause.

McElhone looked tired. The day had been spent staging an elaborate ruse to get Roosevelt into the embassy. An agent had been dressed up as the President and driven through the city with soviet out-riders, while Roosevelt himself had been carried into the embassy from a back door. His legs had dangled like a ventriloquist's dummy.

"Let's talk," said Chainbridge. The delegates were now yelling out toasts.

They went outside. Soviet soldiers formed a perimeter, granite faced. NKVD dressed as waiters flitted in and out. The night was cold, but bearable.

"Here," said McElhone. He handed Chainbridge a photograph. It was an aerial reconnaissance image. It showed a wide grey oval in the middle of a mountain range.

"Urus Martan, or what's left of it."

"How close?"

"The Russians are saying nothing, but it was very, very close."

Chainbridge handed the photograph back. Once it had been developed, it would have been flown transatlantic for the Pentagon to review. Every allied agency would have one by now.

"No doubt, the Abwehr would have a copy of their own to peruse," said Chainbridge.

"I hope so."

"There was a rumour about German paratroopers landing here?"

"It was just a rumour, Henry. The soviets have this place locked down."

Chainbridge opened his Russian cigarette case and offered one to McElhone.

"Peter de Witte thinks there's an American senator involved in this," he glanced around but was satisfied they weren't being overheard. "I've forwarded on the salient details."

"We'll check it out. How is Peter?"

"In Lisbon; following a lead."

"He's got balls; I'll give him that – any word from your team?"

"They're back in Switzerland. We lost three of them."

Chainbridge, despite himself, had a catch in his throat; Brandt, Bader and Olga.

It was the end of the irregulars. End of the adventure.

His thoughts drifted to Eva.

"Thank them for us," said McElhone.

"I will," replied Chainbridge.

A dinner gong was rung. The waiters moved about with greater intensity. Chainbridge could see they were carrying side arms.

"Churchill wants a security briefing."

"Good luck with that," said McElhone.

Chainbridge savoured the last few drags of his cigarette then stubbed it out with his shiny patent leather shoe.

They shook hands and went into the embassy mixing with the crush of uniforms. Stalin was there in his immaculate white Marshall's uniform, ebullient toward Roosevelt. The perfect host.

Chainbridge could see Commissar, 2nd rank of the Soviet Supreme General Staff, Valery Yvetchenko. He caught his eye and raised a glass of vodka.

The Commissar returned the briefest of nods, then mingled with the Russian delegation.

Chainbridge retired to his quarters, checking every nook and cranny for microphones. Amid copies of newspapers and periodicals he found a hand-written note from Curran;

"Henry, nape tide high in the Orkney's – come visit. Note the iniquities of Eve".

Curran's hatred of Eva was coming along nicely, he thought. Seems Int. 7 had uncovered something interesting and off-the-books.

THIRTY ONE.
Switzerland

It had been almost a year since they had been to the modest pension off a quiet side street in Zurich. The apple-cheeked land lady, Mrs. Hausmann, greeted them as if they were her own. The handsome German and his pretty girlfriend were treated to a sumptuous breakfast, miraculously varied, despite the modest larder.

As agreed, they never revealed their real names. The pension was paid in advance.

Brandt produced a bottle of Kirsch and handed it to her. Mrs Hausmann whisked it away, followed by her two cats, all twitching tails and rectum.

"You look exhausted, poor dears, here's the key." She said.

Eva took the key. All she wanted was a long bath.

"Thank you," replied Brandt.

"I'll make a dinner and send it up to you."

"You are too kind."

Once in the room, Brandt locked the door. He prised open a floorboard where he stashed his mountaineering equipment and spare gun. Nothing had been disturbed.

"Looks promising."

He slid back a panel beside the bed. Inside was a metal box containing dollars and several un-cut diamonds. Once satisfied these were as they should be, he checked for hidden microphones; lamps, light switches, bookshelf and the radio.

Anything was possible in this day and age.

Eva stripped and began running a bath.

He stopped at the doorway and studied her. Eva was swirling the water with her hand, he watched her muscles play beneath her skin. She was bruised across her shoulders. He planted soft kisses on them.

"They're new."

She stood up and he continued along her neck. Eva turned and kissed him, her eyes full of mischief.

"I think I'll allow you to scrub my back, Captain Brandt."

"My pleasure."

"In English, Brandt."

He silenced her with a kiss.

They bathed together, slept together and when the dawn broke; made love all day...

Eva woke up. She had been dreaming again. She rolled over to the edge of the bed; Mrs. Hausmann's pension was dark, cold and silent.

Brandt's presence was everywhere; the battered copy of *Ulysses* she had given him, the button from one of her blouses that he kept in an envelope, and the contents under the floorboards.

She made herself a coffee and sat at the window watching the world go by.

Then she opened up a floor board. She removed the cash, two diamonds uncut, her false passport and Brandt's Mauser.

Checking it was loaded and clean, she placed in the pocket of her great coat.

She replaced the floorboard and spread a little of the dust over it and looked around the room one more time.

Waiting until it was dark, Eva closed the pension door silently and crept down the stairs. Pressing her ear against Mrs. Hausmann's door, Eva listened.

Satisfied that the landlady was asleep, Eva slid an envelope under the door. Inside it was a large sum of cash and the spare key.

Eva Molenaar decided she was going to find Brandt; her lover, her friend, her mountaineer.

THE END

© 2017 Robert Craven

About the Author

I was born 02/07/66 in Swinton, Manchester. In 1977, the family emigrated to Sydney, Australia and returned to live in Dublin, Ireland in 1979. I have lived there since. I now live in Rush, Co. Dublin. I'm married and have a family.

My first taste of writing was in 1992, when I submitted a short horror story to a speculative fiction magazine, FTL. Titled 'The Chase', it was accepted and published. From that moment, I got the bug.

I had spent nearly a decade playing bass in bands around Dublin and kept tour diaries. From this I made my first attempt at a novel titled 'Vocals preferred / own transport essential.' I finished it in 2003 and sent it out. I received many positive suggestions, but nothing else.

In 2006 I started writing Get Lenin. It took 5 years to finish and was published in 2011, receiving very positive reviews. The sequel 'Zinnman' was then published in 2012. This was followed by A finger of Night, the third in the Eva series, in 2013.

I have had short stories published in three anthologies:

'A communion of blood' a Vampire short published in 'Broken Mirrors Fractured minds' – Vamptasy Press.

'Vodou' in Red Rattle Book's 'Zombie Bites'.

'The Properties of Mercury' in 'Cogs in Time' a Steampunk Anthology, by Crushing Hearts Black Butterfly Publishing.

Twitter link: https://twitter.com/cravenrobert

FB link: https://www.facebook.com/robert.craven.56

Author photograph by Bob Dixon

Bob Dixon photography
https://www.facebook.com/drbobdixon

Printed in Great Britain
by Amazon